CW00421935

ROUGH

A collection of short stories & poems

Samuel Bryant

Copyright © 2022 Samuel Bryant

All rights reserved

The characters and events portrayed in this book are fictitious.
Any similarity to real persons, living or dead, is coincidental and
not intended by the author.

No part of this book may be reproduced, or stored in a retrieval
system, or transmitted in any form or by any means, electronic,
mechanical, photocopying, recording, or otherwise, without
express written permission of the publisher.

ISBN-13: 9798835134052

Printed in Great Britain

CONTENTS

Always For You

Journey

So, let's think about it this way. Those feelings you have
can be communicated. Not down to their root or anything
but we can understand them.

Huh...? ... We should probably keep on going, right? You
and I only have good intentions. For the right cause, one
reason. Life. For it to be rich and valued we have but to
choose who can. Losing that passion, have we? Drawing a
blank is simply the transition. Don't end yours as well...
No matter how often we are reset, our minds do not tamper.
I don't think anyone is keeping notes. We've already been
here twice before and this time I'm still not impressed. You
must stay, please. I can't bear the thought of being alone
again.

I've made up my mind. We're heading in one direction,
without control or insight. I'm empty, I have made my
goodbyes. - I know what you're thinking, but you've got to
trust me, I didn't do anything. I wish I could explain, he is
dead. We're going to be safer together, you better come in.

How did you find this place? Oh, this? We all ran for
shelter, didn't we? Some, yeah, some didn't move on. We
did, and that's why I'm here now. So, what's next? Well,
we have all the time in the world, so slow down. Look

around, you'll find something to fill your time. Find your place and stay there.

CAMERA SHY

Out of sight, out of mind; or so I thought. Everything I captured in my frame was all that mattered. I capture, I move on. But this time was different. She was different. In the middle of blaring noise from the drums and fans, my world was silenced. Our moment was frozen with the soft click of the shutter. I've found you, undisturbed in your world alone. Once I took that photograph it was too late. From there on, you owned my night. In all your glory, I wanted to get close to you. A distracting buzz I'd call it. I didn't need a reason, just a calling. I could see she's got a lot to tell, she seemed out of place. Not on the surface, her moves matched the time without friction, without poise. My mind however was eager like never before. I wanted to see what she sees, share the thoughts that bring a girl like her to a gig like this. For now, she will be blissfully captured for my digestion so perhaps tonight wasn't going to be too bad after all.

Work stayed the same. A flashy crowd of punks foamed in Islington's misery whilst fake heroes sold their sounds every weekend on the dot. It's funny how all these bands manage to rehash the same old angst. I don't care, mind you, I get paid for the action shots. Black and white blurs of a sweaty bassist 'killing it', joy. I just wish I could see her again; it was like the swarm parted around her and all that was left was a real cause, someone who needed saving and didn't need to cry about it. How come you always have the right words just that one second too late? Fading towards my flat, I messed around in my jeans, flipped for the keys and rocked over to notice Miriam sat up at this time watching QVC; A ton of shite for £21.99. Sad. I can witness in real-time someone giving up on life, sinking into her settee from the cold blue glare. Unfortunately, the old woman noticed me too. As I slugged into the foyer, locking the front door, I ignored her 1 am welcome and refused to turn and acknowledge the routine. To be honest, I should have cut her some slack. Miriam was the kind of neighbour most people would hope for. She'd often pop round to see how you're coping, as well as keep an eye out for the latest chart-topper at Woollies.

Before I know it, I'm prying myself awake again. I can't stop myself from flicking through her images, my dream girl. Morning glory obviously won't forget her any time soon. Work's in twenty minutes and I'm still sitting in this empty flat. Is it always going to feel this empty?

Wake up, get coffee. Ah, yes, that's what I forgot to pick up after work. Too distracted for my own needs, aren't I?

Down the road, there's a new coffee house opening; one of those American chains. It's on the way, so I'll quickly nip in.

There it is. Roasted hot waiting for me. The early scrambles of suits and sound compound together to create the blandest of scenes. I wasn't quite built for choice upon choice. Coffee is coffee, mornings are shit. The worst of all? £1.65 a cup. I'm not joking. That £1.65 was the biggest mistake of my life. I can't believe it. I don't believe it. Red frizzy bob, last night's makeup, hanging eyes and the ever so slight tilt and posing when she talks. I know very well my thoughts are gearing away from just gawking, but I've found her now. Now the curtain closes, of course, she's half my age. I buy the coffee, I stop feeding the thought and my life will continue down this path. But I need her path: that cracked chalky lips path. The nicotine tips and impulsive dreams. She's coated with trouble, I know, but I'll go to her strange world and... Doe-eyed and cool, she waits for the money. I snap back. Without a word, I hand over the change and have the hot cup pressed into my hands. She holds on for a second longer and like that, one by one, her fingers creak back. It's all so natural for her, surely, she-

'*Photographer?*' My ears prick up as if they already recognise the rumbly voice.

This was the moment my whole body failed me. Eyes glued down to the old caring case, a gangly check-around. All over-cautious, with the rare darting of eye contact, that single glimpse was the invitation. So, I stumble for the best response I can conjure; the right words fall out and drinks at six are planned. How on Earth did I manage that?

She's a drinker all right; says this is her regular. A smoky dim pub, sticky wooden tables and cheap crisps. Nice. I take a second in the bathroom. Christ, they reek. One glance in the mirror, composing myself with what I can;

13

four days on the trot jeans and shirt. Nice. I swing open the gents and to my amazement, the girl's still there. Jessie White, an actor and activist; a volatile cocktail that I can't satisfy.

'*Wait!*' It's already too late.

'*You were at Mambo Taxi's last night?*' She fumbles with my camera carelessly.

It's exciting. Any minute now she'll find it, her lost soul caught on film. My secret flashes wrapped in plastic were kept forever. The pure joy in her is mine… mine, mine, mine. I notice a smile creep out from her; it's telling me her secrets. To my absolute shock, she revels in the discovery. Does she want it? Jessie stares at the digital screen; her images lay bare.

'*I'm beautiful.*' Drops from her lips.

'*Yes… I should-*' I cut myself off as Jessie stands up from the stool. I hang on for more.

'*One more round.*' She commands. I sit.

Another dry stout is slammed in front of me. My spit is still cloying from the last. Though she insists that was last calls. No more words are shared; I struggle with the idea of her coming mine. We're fucked enough now; I love her, but she wants to go. We're outside now. God, it's cold. She knows I like her; I took her picture. I kept it. I let this happen. Blurred yellow lights lead us back. We manage like pinballs on the pavement. The frequent bump of our skin courses through me. I catch my breath each time like a drunk old man wandering around at night.

Somehow, we're here. Hers, not mine. She's brought me into a wall of stench. A squatters place somewhere. My lungs wince from the unfamiliar sogginess. Jessie pulls me past the warm bodies spilt across the hall. Sprayed cries on the walls and tangles of rot seem everywhere. Countless nights swathed in cigs and booze, blankets and mugs, sex and misery. What a fucking place. Forgotten. No. It's been here the whole time; decaying in perfect view, for all to see. This never-ending come down needs gear. So, we keep trekking until her spot; the basement. Jessie crashes onto her mattress. It is plastered with stains but not a flinch of repulsion is made.

'You just gonna stand there or what?' I hesitate at the door frame.

She isn't the obvious choice, a broken girl on coke. There's a fire in her eyes though, which reaches out for me in an erotic ambush. I can't grip the flame; it scorches my insides. A white kiss on the nose. My turn. Knots tauten. What's her story? A crumpled dress in the corner shoved beneath a tainted desk. Red ceiling. The colour ebbs at the corner, and now I notice that continuous buzzing of the bulb. But now there's pain? My body refuses to catch up. Am I drifting away? What the fuck has she done to me? Textured panic creeps in as my vision blurs. But she's not done playing yet. It only takes one sucker punch to knock me down again and rifle through my jeans without thought. I want to give her everything; she needs my protection. I need to just keep my mouth shut, it's what I'm good at. But with every second dragging further than the last it sends another bolt of confirmation between us.

'You got nothing on you?!'

'I'm skint. I'm sorry.'

'Bollocks. Why you lying?'

'It's alright, I'll just get going.'

But she wasn't having it. Jessie fought to climb on top of my chest. Her thighs pressed into my lungs, lurking above me. Open-mouthed and clammy, she raised her hand over me and hit my face. Again, the pulsation ran through me; she must love me. I tried lurching myself off the bed but her will to hold me down dominated my drunken state. Inside the elation cultivated rapidly: could she really find every inch? Just the thought seemed so normal, yet I was very scared. Jessie's gaunt face was a greyish pale. She slid off, hitting the floor. Her body contorted into a foetal position of sorts. A wicked jet of vomit sprayed across her room, coating the flaky plaster with a hot retch. A grizzle of a cry was let out and I eventually shuffle myself off the mattress.

I leave and wash through the rain towards home, sobering along the way. The whirlpool begins its next cycle. Jessie will be laying in her filth, dying. My saviour is alone and all I did was run. I should have caressed her there and then. All this time I've wished for love; someone who needs me. Coffee girl could have been a fantasy that would forever grow. She would hang on to every word, tiptoeing to my spell of secrets. We are lonely people, looking for that fun. But I'm lying to myself if I think I could have found it tonight at the bottom of a glass and a pile of blow. I can't trust myself to hold back from her. She's seeded my mind with pain and all I want to do is go back. I neglected my little sparkle…

I find myself back at the flat, thinking I could kill for a coffee and sleep this mess off. Poor Miriam, I can hear she's still up faffing about. Then in her slippers, dragging across the hall she shuffles towards the door and beckons my company. I oblige. Too late to argue. The fuzzy warmth invites me in like home. The old neighbour sticks the kettle on whilst I make myself welcome, scoffing the tray of biscuits next to the settee. She's helping the wrong guy for the right reasons, bless. My legs give way and I relax.

'You had a busy night then?'

'One I'll soon forget, hopefully. I'm shattered.'

'Is everything okay at work? Not a money problem again, is it?'

The frankness of that last comment lingers. Poor thing doesn't deserve getting involved. Miriam struggles to set down both mugs, spilling a few drops of tea on the coaster. I'm prompted to take one, regrettably finding tea in mine as well. I stretch a smile anyway. Sitting back down, Miriam and I go over the usual stuff, she comforts me with her reassuring manner yet straightforward approach. All this time she glosses over the glaring state I'm in. Maybe I want her to notice something is wrong? Either way, we buckle in for more late-night shopping.

'Where'd I leave my bag, Miriam?'

'Silly, you didn't bring anything with you. Must be in your room.'

No. Not my 'room'… And just like that, a familiar face emerges.

'*Am I a fucking joke to you?!*' Splutters from outside. My ears prick up and I see Jessie wiping her lips with her sleeve. Our night's despair blotted across her chest. Perfect.

'*I beg your pardon? How dare you!*' Shouts Miriam.

Jessie doesn't hesitate to offload around the flat; she's probably still smashed.

'*You're okay.*' I perk.

'*No thanks to you, dickhead.*' Thrown back, like a knife.

'*What the Devil is going on?*'

'*I ain't got time for this love. I need sorting.*' Jessie still stumbled around with authority.

Miriam is pushed to the ground, shrieking as she falls. Her head impacts the table, shattering its ornaments. There's a palpable moment of complete silence. I can't process it, just a dreed of complete denial fills me and surely Jessie as she stands over her fixating her gaze. How did it escalate to this?

'*Fucking hell... Is she?*' I literally can't say it.

Jessie doesn't respond. She steps over Miriam, turns to me and lays her head into my neck. Slowly lulling herself in my arms. Time waits for us to form a plan. Jessie whispers her torments to me. I share them now. Before too long, a stash of rubber-banded tenners are discovered in her bedroom. Jessie doesn't bother counting and stuffs them down her top. The crusty numbness of tiredness leaves.

'*You coming, then?*'

Abandoning that once warming brew as the television was left buzzing, I made my decision. A part of me was left behind at the scene of the crime, and as it left me, maybe in some desperate act of redemption, it knocked the home telephone onto the floor. Maybe it wanted to let her know I was sorry, for I am the fool.

A fool who followed in the wake of Jessie's chaos. To be

honest, would I change a thing?

Death's Dilemma

Let me paint you a picture. For five thousand years now
I've been judge, jury and executioner for the humans of
Earth. I've seen the soul take many forms, some of which
had even worshipped me. Today though is different. Today
I stumbled, I was not prepared, and to be honest with you…
I don't have the answer.

You see, humans, they think they got it going pretty well
for themselves, well not all of them. Someone had to tinker
and test to see how far they could push me. I'm a pretty
transparent guy so I made it clear to upstairs that
technology and even all this medicine, had to slow down.

Well, eventually things became less and less clear. We had
surgeons, comas, bionics… I could take that, I could draw
the line. But when I started seeing those machines
moving… feeling… living… A part of me died.

"I can't kill them", that's what I told myself at first. But I
had to. By the nature of law, these bolts had a brain and a
heart and they finally found a soul. Mother nature had her
hands already full with the rest of our survival situation.
Now, new creatures were created too soon, no biological
evolution could create such an event, such a corruption.

I came to my senses once I realised this "A-I" was not self-
renewable and well let's face it, they can't die… right?

Surely it wasn't my job to do anything with them, throw 'em in the trash. Well like I said, they had souls. Fuck. Somehow that was almost a replica of the blueprint of humans. I mean what else could they go by at this point? They oh so loved to colonise but apparently, it was time to play God now.

But like I said, almost. Humans couldn't harness the purity of the soul. The maker's heart came from a developed, tainted place. They wanted purpose, they wanted to control.

They thought to birth the bolts with knowledge instead of tools. With this as their foundation, the entire production was at risk.

So here we are today, again. Yes even now after hearing my story will you begin life here, I guess this is your...

>HEAVEN []

>HELL []

An Untitled Collection

We dispel our foes into the darkness, for just a moment.
Weaving our hearts together. Dreaming down, further into
no land, a place that you accept and always have.

———

I'm still looking for you, chances are you aren't there. All I
think about is your hair, and your voice at times. locked out
until that reunion. The world had its pace that was unfit for
you and me. But we don't have the world at our side now,
do we?

———

Still thy love. The ease has been found in our power… of
hate. We shall continue down this path with vengeance.

The system will fail you, without a trace to argue with. One
by one you are denied! Ignoring the human presence that
still remains.

———

Evil has stolen all beauty.

All that is beautiful is gone.

Owned by the top and wrong of the land.

—

Perhaps some time has passed, and now, in this time we can conclude what has been. The mess can settle down with fresh words to witness the world that has become. Each step away from the horror leads to the unknown, could that tale be our last step? Ravelled in a home, too tangled to see reality, we begin anew. We try, try again. Butting heads against the perceived backdrop. This trick cannot fool twice!

Our condition brings an old experience, a choice to reopen the scab that itches you. It itches and pulls, growing inside you. Under the surface. To ignore is your weapon, and with time looming behind ever so closer.

These feelings have their own time, their own space in your memory, a place that is forever occupied by what you have witnessed, this cannot be undone. The next plane has always been waiting, the wrong hands will no longer spread its web.

Pull. Pull again, because forever this will be your fate. The dead only have you to entertain.

And here it goes. Your spirit will not accept the lies you hopelessly wish to spin.

ASHES

CAST

THE HUNTER: A ruthless mercenary

THE COLLECTOR: An educated 'WITCH'-
finder

'WITCH': A cunning traveller

"ASHES"

FADE IN:
EXT. OPEN ROAD - MORNING
A prisoner wagon is driven on a barren
road in the early hours. The morning
mist licks the wheels and blankets the
open land, autumn themes the trees; a
golden bask of light. Its two drivers,
bounty collectors, are returning from a
mission to find the wanted 'WITCH'.

                    THE HUNTER

Bloody hell, she reeks!

                    THE COLLECTOR

Disgusting little things, aren't they?

THE HUNTER

Bastard demons. Don't know what's good
for 'em. (pause)
Go on then, what'd she have on her?

(THE COLLECTOR rummages through a large
pouch on his lap, he darts his eyes to
see if THE HUNTER notices him pocketing
a few coins.)

THE COLLECTOR

Quite… Some cherries, bread and what
else do we have here?
(pause)

THE HUNTER

Give it 'ere, let's 'ave a look!

(THE HUNTER leans over and attempts to
snatch the pouch and almost takes the
wagon off-road, horses let out a neigh.)

31

THE COLLECTOR

Watch it, you brute! Do you want to get
us killed over a rotten loaf?

(THE HUNTER doesn't respond to THE
COLLECTOR and whips the horses.)

Now, if you give me a moment, I will be
able to inspect our prize.

(THE COLLECTOR places the pouch in the
footwell. Behind him sits a young girl,
curled up in the wagon's cage. She sits
in the furthest corner from the two men,
her head in between her knees. THE
COLLECTOR attempts to gain 'WITCH''s
attention by looking over his shoulder
and proclaiming.)

THE COLLECTOR (CONT'D)

No coin.

(For a moment 'WITCH' looks up and the
two catch each other's attention,
quickly she turns her head away and
looks out to the road.)

THE HUNTER

Bah!

THE COLLECTOR

But perhaps this piece will fetch a high price.

THE HUNTER

Eh?

THE COLLECTOR

We have ourselves a thief and a 'WITCH'!

THE HUNTER

But we only got one girl back there.

THE COLLECTOR

No, you idiot. That 'WITCH' stole this.

(THE COLLECTOR pulls out a handmade
trinket and rattles it against the bars
of the cage. 'WITCH' squints her brow
and is visibly worried, she begins to
shuffle towards the front of her cage
without alerting the two men.)

THE HUNTER

Maybe now, we'll get more coin for her?

THE COLLECTOR

No… A 'WITCH', a 'WITCH'. A thief all
the same.

THE HUNTER

Too bad her little band ran off then?

THE COLLECTOR

Bah. Don't worry about them, she'll tell
us in due part. And when she does, we'll
be heading straight back out here, won't
we?

THE HUNTER

Yeah! We'll get every one of yers!

(Directing at 'WITCH'.)

You heard, bitch.

THE COLLECTOR

You waste your breath. Simple creatures.
But like all problems, a pest that
doesn't give up-

(Cut off)

'WITCH'

Simple?

(Both THE HUNTER AND THE COLLECTOR turn around.)

THE HUNTER

It talks?!

THE COLLECTOR

Nay do not be fooled.

THE HUNTER

You hear that though? I've never heard 'em speak before.

(THE COLLECTOR does not respond, still turned he glares at the 'WITCH', leans slowly and lets out a large exhale.)

THE COLLECTOR

You have something to say? Go on speak.
Speak for me.

(pause)

(THE HUNTER looks over his shoulder with
a sneering grin. In his hand, THE
COLLECTOR holds a tattered book open.
Loose pieces of note paper slip out from
between the pages.)

What a shame. It almost had a thought,
but no. The senseless creature waits for
us to clean its mess-
(Cut off)

('WITCH' is staring with contempt.)

THE HUNTER

And those, what are they? Incantations?
That there is evil.

(THE HUNTER jabs his finger into the
book, THE COLLECTOR sighs from being cut

off again.)

THE COLLECTOR

How are we to know? I let the Crown deal
with that problem. (pause)Is it possible
this dreadful farce all comes down to a
(pause) mistake?

THE HUNTER

What? I go through all the trouble of
coming out to fuck knows where to drag a
girl all the way back to town just to be
told from some capital guard 'Thanks
lads, we'll handle it from here'. No. We
are doing this for good reason. Not just
bloody coin. Our people are picked off
one by one and most are afraid to even
speak of this horror that we see each
day. (Pause) This has to be done.

THE COLLECTOR

But do you question our great
protectors? The powers which stop the
spread of such evil.

THE HUNTER

I do question such. You seen their evil
before?

THE COLLECTOR

Of course! I never told of my escape
from their bladed beasts?

(A flock of crows fly off from the edges
of the woods in the distance. Disturbed
by a sound deeper in the woods. Both
turn in the direction of the shriek.)

THE HUNTER

Somethin' you couldn't face?

THE COLLECTOR

It was no matter of could. This creature
was far beyond any hunt. (pause) Damn.

(THE COLLECTOR looks out to the woods
ahead and they begin to creep over the
rolling hill. He whips off his leather
gloves and clasps his hands, soothing

himself by rocking forward.)

THE HUNTER

Do tell!

THE COLLECTOR

Ah, well our journey is far from over so
I guess I can give free rein to my
tales. You see, away from our towns of
filth and struggle there is much to
learn. Before I joined the Crown's
collectors, I had studied 'WITCH'es for
many years, (pause) to understand their
way, (pause) to try and reason with such
evil.

(THE COLLECTOR's speech whittles away to
almost a whisper.)

THE HUNTER

So, you thought, you'd come out here for
blood instead?

(A grimace curl of the lips appears on
THE HUNTER's face, there is no attempt
to hide his glee.)

THE COLLECTOR

More than blood my friend, much much
more!

(As the woods come into view from the
side of the track the 'WITCH' looks up
with a similar glee to THE HUNTER.)

THE COLLECTOR (CONT'D)

The shadows these witches cast blanket
our very ways, they drift man's minds to
cripple and ruin what they build.

THE HUNTER

That's all women, ain't it?

THE COLLECTOR

You would want to believe that? Too easy
is the trap of power. I find out there,
something I cannot explain.

CUT TO EXT. SPARSE WOODLAND - DAY

THE COLLECTOR is alone wandering through the usual trail. In his hand, he rubs a leaf and brings it to his nose. Smiling at the pleasant and familiar smell he stops, crouches down and inspects the shrubbery at his feet.

                 THE COLLECTOR (CONT'D) O.S.

One morn as I collected berries deep in thy a flock emerged out from the shadows. I tell you, I be surrounded by them.

CUT TO EXT. OPEN ROAD - MORNING

The wagon now rides on the fringes of the wood.

                      THE HUNTER

Must 'a wanted to make jam for their bread?

(THE HUNTER lets out a hearty laugh to himself along with a whip to the horses.)

CUT TO EXT. SPARSE WOODLAND - DAY

THE COLLECTOR O.S.

I wish! Their intentions were made clear
soon enough, one drew her blade and
ordered the rest to retreat. Without a
word they vanished. I readied myself to
run.
(pause)

(THE COLLECTOR, unarmed, sees that his
path out is blocked. His body stiffens.
The frontman is equipped with a rusted
hoe blade, a perfectly kept black robe
hides his face. His rolled-up sleeves
display a collection of scars and dirt
which cover most of their arms.)

THE COLLECTOR (CONT'D) OFF-SCREEN

I froze. And next to this he-'WITCH'
stood a beast. A blade upon its head and
as dark as the shadows from whence the
others came.

(Interjects)

CUT TO EXT. OPEN ROAD - MORNING

THE HUNTER (MIMICKING)

A blade upon its head, ha!

THE COLLECTOR

You laugh easily now fool, this stallion
stood taller than any I had seen, easily
twice the size of these two.

(Points at horses.)

THE HUNTER

And this horse? It just stared. You must
have dropped ya berries.

THE COLLECTOR

You don't understand! These witches were
different, that horn must be special to
them. Special enough to create this.

(Shows trinket to 'WITCH', she shuffles
forward.)

Bah, stay back!

'WITCH'

You are wrong.

(THE HUNTER holds up the horses)

THE HUNTER

Woah, easy, easy now.
(pause)
What's she on about?

THE COLLECTOR

Yes, do tell.

'WITCH'

Those were no 'WITCH'es.

THE COLLECTOR

Ah, how wise, however could we be

tricked?

                    'WITCH'

Would you listen-

('WITCH' climbs to her feet, pulling her
weak body up with the support of the
cage, THE HUNTER bangs on the bars.
'WITCH' panics, drops down and is cut
off.)

                  THE HUNTER

Shut it you. We've got a long road
ahead, and I ain't listening to some
rubbish about some sorry traveller you
had to pinch from.

(THE COLLECTOR leans in and whispers to
THE HUNTER)

                 THE COLLECTOR

Don't you care to learn of her… powers?

THE HUNTER

What you on about?

THE COLLECTOR

Surely a group with such beast at their side muster knowledge we have yet to take?

'WITCH'

You take everything, and still, you want more.

THE COLLECTOR

Twisting that young one? You are in your cage only for the very nature of the greed and suffering you plague our lives with.

'WITCH'

Says the one holding my pouch.

THE HUNTER

You own nothing, never have, girl! Our
land has enough problems, can't you stay
where you belong?

(Thick clouds form above, and the warm
morning glow fades into a dark cast.
Further up the steep road, showers can
be seen covering their path. The
horrible weather makes it difficult to
see and hear. The cart drifts off the
path.)

'WITCH'

And where do 'we' belong?

THE HUNTER

Not 'ere!

'WITCH'

Yes…

THE COLLECTOR

Tell me, the lead 'WITCH', where is he
now?

'WITCH'

I serve no leader, verily no 'WITCH'es.

THE COLLECTOR

That band of girls back there was not
your coven?

'WITCH'

I know such of a coven, however, that
does not concern I.

THE HUNTER

You're all the same…

'WITCH'

My fate was sealed I suppose once I was
cursed.

THE COLLECTOR

A curse?

'WITCH'

Yes, by said he-'WITCH' no less. In
Sarple markets this summer I worked.

THE COLLECTOR

Yes, I know of them. You get a good
price for their cheeses.

THE HUNTER

Sarple cheese? naff stuff. All about
that Bosbury local.

                    'WITCH'

Simple…

                THE COLLECTOR

You were saying?

                    'WITCH'

The Sarple markets are packed with
worldly travellers and treats you could
never dream of. I remember one stall, an
elder sat patiently. In front he had
placed a simple box, children would
often run by and snatch the thing
wanting to find its surprise for
themselves. Funnily enough, they always
returned saddened and sorry with the box
in hand.

                THE HUNTER

What's in the box?

'WITCH'

Well you see opening the box is no easy
task, the elder tells that he waits for
the one to finally come and enlighten
the world of what it holds.

THE COLLECTOR

What could be so precious?

'WITCH'

I can tell if you truly wish.

(THE HUNTER and THE COLLECTOR turn to
see 'WITCH' reaction; she lets out a
smile. THE HUNTER looks around to get
his bearings, he doesn't wish to scare
the other two.)

I tried my luck one day before work, the
elder arrives before anyone else, no one
remembers when he first came. I thought,
how strange for me to work so long and
yet never approach such a thing. Once I
did, I took a good look at the old man,
he did not welcome me.

THE HUNTER

The old man knew a 'WITCH'.

'WITCH'

I wavered to pick up such mystery, why bother when so many have failed?

THE COLLECTOR

You did not fail though?

'WITCH'

Fail… No.

FADE TO EXT. MARKET STALL - DAWN

A younger 'WITCH' towers over an old dusty traveller. The man is crossed-legged surrounded by his exotic and colourful wares. Priceless yet strange relics that appear to have no significant value. The sun is only starting to creep over the houses, casting a ray directly in front of the old man. The young 'WITCH' is intrigued by the ornate square box that rests at his battered feet. She remembers the whispers and tales from passers-by and children. The riches it holds, the evil it guards. All considered, she casts aside her reasoning and weighs up the man's sincerity.

'WITCH' (CONT'D) O.S.

He simply waited, looking up at me with his blank face.

('WITCH' kneels and turns the box around, darting between a reaction from its owner and for a latch to open it. The man places both his hands over hers, she pauses to see a glowing smile encase her with warmth and ease.)

Opening the box was no prize for me. A terrible shriek was let out that very moment. I was swarmed almost in an instant. I could only see the street children gasping at the edges of the swarm, a hand escaped the crowd and reached for me, snatching the open box. 'Thief, thief, a 'WITCH' has cursed us!'. They saw a lonely girl and knew.

FADE TO EXT. STEEP WINDING ROAD — DARK AND DRIZZLY AFTERNOON

THE HUNTER

What curse was on them?

'WITCH'

No curse, I was the change they did not welcome.

THE COLLECTOR

They were quick to find a 'WITCH'.

'WITCH'

But I was quicker! I knew my life would
surely meet its end if I waited to see a
blade turned inward. One blade did not,
still, another arm pulled me under the
crowd. A gipsy of sort short tells of
safety out of town, soon the Crown guard
would fall upon its so-called duty.

THE HUNTER

That gipsy saved your skin.

'WITCH'

Yes, we quickly made leave to her
caravan.

THE COLLECTOR

You moved out here?!

'WITCH'

Where was I supposed to live?
(pause)

THE HUNTER

They were gipsies?
(directed at THE COLLECTOR.)

THE COLLECTOR

Maybe.

THE HUNTER

You told me, 'WITCH'es!

(THE HUNTER stops the wagon and gets off
to go to the back and confront 'WITCH'.)

What are you playing us for? Huh?

'WITCH'

I told you I'm not a-

THE COLLECTOR

Oy! Leave her alone.

THE HUNTER

What?! You believe her hex?

(THE HUNTER storms over to THE COLLECTOR
still sat.)

Give me that.

(THE HUNTER and THE COLLECTOR struggle
over the pouch, THE HUNTER punches THE
COLLECTOR.)

Explain!
(wafts trinket)
(pause)

I said explain!
(shorter pause)

'WITCH'

It is my weapon.

THE HUNTER

Is it magic? Is this what you steal from
a poor man?

'WITCH'

It protects witches.

THE COLLECTOR

Stop this.

(The trinket's emerald appearance begins
to fade to a ruby red, as it is wafted
again. Unbeknownst to the men. The
'WITCH' looks on in fright and shoots up
once more.)

THE HUNTER

Shut it! This. This thing is from that
beast, no?

'WITCH'

Yes.

(THE HUNTER taps the bars of the wagon
with the trinket and drops it to the
floor, he begins to stamp on it.)

                    THE HUNTER

Will it protect you, eh 'WITCH'? It
doesn't seem like you're a strong
'WITCH'.

                  THE COLLECTOR

What are you doing?!

(THE COLLECTOR climbs down holding his
nose, bleeding.)

                    THE HUNTER

She admits! Her power is in this thing.

                  THE COLLECTOR

You idiot?! What are we supposed to
bring to the Crown?!

THE HUNTER

The `WITCH'!

THE COLLECTOR

For all we now know, this girl is a
gipsy that we have kidnapped!
(pause)

THE HUNTER

Oh, I get it. You want to save the bitch
now? Here, `WITCH', have it back.

(THE HUNTER picks up a pile of dust
along with a fragment of the trinket and
blows it into her face causing her to
splutter. She stands defiant in her pose
and gaze.)

THE COLLECTOR

What now?

(THE HUNTER returns to the front of the
wagon for his weapon and keys)

THE HUNTER

Alright, 'WITCH', you want to prove
yourself?

THE COLLECTOR

Now, this is ridiculous. You can't do
this.

(THE HUNTER walks past THE COLLECTOR and
leans in close to him.)

THE HUNTER

Stop me.

(THE HUNTER unlocks the prison wagon and
swings it open.)

Come out here and show me what your
worth, good coin or just blood.

THE COLLECTOR O.S.

If you-

(THE HUNTER points his sword towards THE
COLLECTOR.)

                 THE HUNTER

Disgusting little things, aren't they?
(pause)

('WITCH' makes a run for it and jumps
out of the wagon grabbing the trinket
and pouch from THE HUNTER.)

'WITCH'!

(THE HUNTER runs after her, THE
COLLECTOR stands still and looks around
panicking.)

                THE COLLECTOR

No, no, no, no, no.

EXT. ENTRANCE OF WOODS - DARK AFTERNOON

(Cut to 'WITCH' running and not looking

back.)

                THE HUNTER O.S.

Keep running, I won't stop!

('WITCH' gets closer to the edge of the
woods and turns to run towards them, THE
HUNTER holsters his sword and goes into
a full sprint. THE HUNTER shortens the
gap and begins to slow down as he loses
track once he enters the woods. THE
HUNTER stops to look around and pants
heavily). THE HUNTER's hip dagger is
drawn and quickly thrust into his neck
by 'WITCH', he turns to see her and
grabs his throat choking and staggering
slowly towards her. THE HUNTER falls
face down moments later. 'WITCH' is
shaking, she unsheathes his blade.)

(THE COLLECTOR is sitting on the wagon,
the horses nibble at the grass at the
side of the road, he aches in pain from
the earlier punch, THE COLLECTOR lets in
a sharp breath.)

EXT. OPEN ROAD #3 - DAY

THE COLLECTOR

Big bastard's going to get us both
killed.

('WITCH' returns and throws down THE
HUNTER's sword on the floor next to
him.)

THE COLLECTOR

Wh-What happened?

'WITCH'

I would leave as soon as you can.

THE COLLECTOR

What do you mean… you didn't?

(THE COLLECTOR stops himself and looks
towards the woods.)

'WITCH'

Please, be my guest.
('WITCH' goes over to the horses and

strokes them.)

'WITCH' (CONT'D)

So, am a 'WITCH', am I?

THE COLLECTOR

You're a murderer!

'WITCH'

I'm whatever you tell them. Pity.

('WITCH' untangles the horses, letting
them free to run.)

THE COLLECTOR

Where are you-

'WITCH'

Here.

('WITCH' throws pouch at THE COLLECTOR)

There's your prize.

('WITCH' leaves THE COLLECTOR and the
empty wagon.)

FADE OUT.

Shock

"Nothing quite like family. I know they can't wait to see me home. Can't believe the photo survived as well."

Jack removes a fresh cigar from his smoking jacket. His journey over the Atlantic is almost silent, the duties of war have finally come to an end.

A flash of light blinds Jack from the passenger window, suddenly smoke fills the aircraft, choking the air and further blinding his vision. Plummeting into the ocean below, Jack is thrown into the exit passage, his conscious now leaving. With a last-ditch effort, he swings open the door, sucked out and into the ocean alone.

I'm supposed to be on one of those documentaries, I survived. I have a life. This is the music. What is happening?

Art is on the floor, waiting for you. All.

Your ocean is my ocean

All the efforts have brought me here because they are mine.
We can both stand by our losses, but now you shall call this
place home for the rest of your days.

Short. Shorter. Longest. You already know how crucial
your time is. How and well more importantly with who. I
can't tell how long it truly has been and oh how long I can
really take wasting away... An isle rich with life and
colour, a life that ignores my cries every night. The shore
now holds those nights captor.

At the other end, home. Home still exists, right? Why. Why
have I not walked into the dark? The cold will embrace me.
I will be accepted finally. The wrap, the crash. I want this.

Let me want the simple life. I am with nature, no? I will
never unlearn of my heaven.

I don't like fish. They are numbing to swallow. To know
how each day will unfold is my true horror.

I can no longer learn. I just can't. I want a teacher, someone
just to tell me when I am wrong. Lost. Can anyone else be
lost? The cliffs will not hold my tale. No, a tragedy, I could
end it, but hope is my friend, a corner in my mind, just out
of reach darkness bleeds, suggesting in infinite terrors and
dreams. Drawing you.

I cannot be alone. I know I heard someone, just as I start to drift. They sound close, taking their time. It frightens me. I am frozen.

No. No. No. No.

Folk

I t was a desolate town where a small number of houses and abandoned stores lined the dirt road. Many had moved on to better lives and bigger dreams. Though few hung around, clinging to this dustbowl home; pining for customers when a mere traveller would pass through. The western storms were ending the normal for every town that had succumbed to the ever-growing clouds, people were no longer living but surviving.

Only the Herald brothers remained. The eldest of the two, fashioned in his father's red velvet two-piece, a revolutionary salesman and famed for his medical wisdom and wonderous treatments for the ill. For the young, bottled elephant blood for vim and vigour! For the old, iron

tobacco for strength like never before! The doctor was

never short of meeting the demands of all who passed

through the once vibrant market. On the other side of town,

the younger brother, a banker, made quick work of loans

for the needy, dodging the small print and without

questioning their circumstance. Travellers would often

arrive with trouble. Somewhere safe to keep their coin from

bandits or needing a handful of money to help them on

their way. This was where the youngest of the two took

pride in his work.

Supplies now running thin and no longer can the

two rely on new travellers passing on through. Dawn began

to break and already Jack had found a coffee jar still laying

around the sheriff's office. He paused to take a good look

around the ransacked heap of documents, the empty cells,

all a forgotten home.

Out on the porch the air felt cold despite the sun burning above, the dust swept through the entrance catching Jack's throat, he lets out a mean cough and regains his posture with the reception desk. Ron leaned against the windowpane and scanned the outside strip, his eyes tracked his struggling brother coming down from the porch opposite, still clutching at his shirt and with a well-balanced jar underneath his arm. Ron let out a wheezy chortle and made his way out onto the sweltering sun, allowing himself to be far too smug for his surroundings to permit.

'*Ya supposed to boil 'em first!*' Jack made out, he perked his head up to see his brother cleaning his lenses with a handkerchief. Ron nodded his head in the direction of the bar, on the quieter side of town.

Jack clears his throat before responding, *'Nothing too stiff, Ron. Thought I'd treat us to a fresh start.'*

Ron steps back inside to unload his medical bag for possible visitors. The saloon had not long been abandoned, a room where barmaids would dance between drunkards with soft laughter now stood as an example of the result of the billowing storms that had swept in a blanket of dust. The air was thick, and the scent of liquor no longer clung to the walls, all that was left was the eerie silence. As the brothers began to dust off a set of barstools to sit upon, Ron's attention was drawn elsewhere as he took a glance out of the dirtied window.

Upon the horizon, a flickering haze came into view; a lone figure now stood along with their large black steed waiting patiently further back near the bank. Ron abandoned his stool and made his way over to the window, squinting to see through the dust-stained glass. An older gentleman dressed in black from head to toe ventured towards the saloon, dust clouds forming at his feet and clinging to any fabric it contacted. Once he was a few steps away from the saloon, he stopped and began to speak aloud, though the brothers had not stepped out, into his sight.

'Your garden shall never grow, nor even bare the suggestion. What sort of monsters would uproot the very ground that is such a necessity?'

The minister continues his volley as the brothers weigh up the performance, deciding that it was best to make their way out of the building.

'What's wrong with that horse? Can't she stand damn still?' Ron finally steps across the porch to inspect his horse, the visitor pulls at the reigns abruptly, causing the horse to whip its head.

The gentleman continues *'Where? Where is she? I don't have any money. I know she keeps asking. I'm sick of hearing this. Just tell me where to go. But it is too much, I didn't want to. I'm hurt.'*

Jack interrupts, *'Sir? You need to turn around and go back to where you came.'*

'I need to go. But you haven't told them yet. Who's going to pay me? Work out here, no?' continues the man without hesitation.

'What are you yapping on about? We don't need no more drunks, this bar has long gone.' Ron demands the man to leave but his words keep spilling out.

Both brothers stand aside one another, taking up the mannerisms of their late mother as their hands sat upon their hips as they both squinted towards the rambling stranger.

'You see, I've got to get there, they're waiting for me. And she…she just won't stop, you see.' The minister nodded his head as though trying to direct the brother's attention to the individual he spoke of. With the impatience of his father, the doctor let out a huff and took his leave, making his way back to the chemist.

'Yer not gonna make it far, the storms been brewing up a fuss.' The banker spoke out in a bellowing voice, though the stranger continued to mutter to himself.

The minister began to pace, circling the area between the saloon and the bank which stood parallel; thick dust following his direction.

'Now, I'm a man of God and thou shall not sin. But I didn't mean no harm…my conscious is clean. I declare it!' The man came to a halt, his fists balled up so rightly that his battered knuckles began to weep.

'Oh…but my sweet girl…she looked so

scared…as though the Devil himself stood before her!'

The remaining brother stood. As though an audience to this one-man charade, though no cheers were called out at the act, the sound was replaced by a hoarse cough as the dust began to catch in his throat.

'Ah! Thank you, good sir! I do bid you good

day." the minister abruptly called.

And as quickly as the strange figure entered this town, he made his exit. Though the banker hadn't offered him any sort of direction of where to go.

Dumbfounded, Jack turns on his heels and makes his way to the chemist where Ron had stormed off to. His stomach gave a churning growl and a cold wave rippled throughout him, causing his hairs to stand on end, though he brushed this off to be the lack of breakfast and hoped the feeling would subside.

Just as he came to the chemist doors, a thunder of galloping echoed across town, causing Jack to turn back to where he'd come. His face squeezed into a tight stare, a blemish of ginger dust clinging to the curl of his moustache. Not another moment passes, and Jack's attention is swung to the other end of town.

Suddenly, Ron appears, pulling his brother out from the road just as a large wagon races by, causing Jack to lose balance and fall to the ground. The wagon is made up of half shrubbery and splintered wood. It grinds to a halt as the horses let out a piercing cry, the owners of which seem unfazed.

'Sorry about that! We must have gotten carried away, isn't that right, dear?' The female passenger leans out to inspect any damage.

'Ma'am. You gotta look where you're headin'. I know it ain't the busiest of towns but that's my brother you see here.' Ron spoke out, over the huffing breaths of the horses. Towering over him sat a young married couple in their well-fashioned dress.

From the doorway, legs laced in white descended, though the dampened mud spoils the perfect fabric. The woman's partner looks over to see the introductions and remains seated further griping the reins before asking,

'Please don't. Not now. Think of the children, they wouldn't want us to be squandering out in nowhere.' *Oh, aren't these two dressed for the occasion, maybe I shouldn't be so kind to two young gentlemen on my honeymoon, now should I?'* the bride's response perks the ears of the brothers to attention.

'You two lovebirds must be having quite the trip seeing the state of your wagon.' Jack's scrutiny is ignored, these two didn't look like they were settling for the night.

'So, you new around these parts?' Ron interjects.

The groom stares at Jack.

'No Ron, don't you remember 'em? Last Summer, now what was it? You were looking at loans for a nurse, right? Ya kid needed supervisin'.' The woman focuses on sifting through their trunk. Again, to the surprise of the brothers, these visitors are preoccupied with themselves rather than looking for a pitstop.

'Pol, darlin', where are they?' The husband makes out, genuinely confused.

'With my ma, how many times do I have to explain?'

The husband climbs down from his wagon and embraces his wife, lifting his hands into her hair and combing through her bun, ever so slightly loosening it with each stroke. His hands are covered in scratches, the skin is swollen from impact and possibly fatigue. Only now do the brothers notice her dress is ripped at most seams.

'My sweet sugar plum...' the man sang into his lover's ear whilst his bride swayed in his arms, their affection growing almost sickly.

The woman's face was one of tranquillity, though the hint of annoyance ripples across her glare.

'Our sweet children, where did you take them?' the way he spoke was as though reciting a spell, trying to coax the truth from his wife.

'I left them with mother!' she snapped, though instead of pulling away, her hands which were scratched to

ribbons clutched her husband's arms tighter, her nails threatening to break his skin.

'We needed a break; they were so noisy...such a nuisance...those brats.' A poisonous spit is made with each pause and her pretty face twists from the previous soft-blushed cheeks.

After a moment's silence, the brothers lingering with a stance of awkwardness, one spoke.

'You two must take something for the road ahead.'

Ron opens up his depleting trunk of bottles and boxes which roll and clunk in a satisfying action. He dips into the bag and pulls out a creamy concoction that is peddled to protect travellers, knowingly traded in market towns like such.

Without a mention of price, the husband rummages in his pockets for all the money he has and empties it into the doctor's hand, coins fall to the ground and quickly Ron squats to pick at them. As he stands, the newlyweds are already setting off. A lack of exchange in words leaves the brothers to examine the back of the wagon, a small arm hung limply from between the doors, a scrap of cloth which appeared to be from the woman's dress held tightly in its frozen grasp. Jack bursts to catch their attention but it is futile as the horse pace into a gallop and is left to disperse into the horizon once more, disappearing into the sea of ever-growing dust.

'Jack, take a look at this!' Ron shouts his brother over; he cradles the egregious load that has been offered in return for a measly bottle of pop.

'You won't believe how much they had on 'em. Fools! We could set up shop in the capital with this kind of luck.'

Jack rushes back to the bank and begins to shuffle through a large stack of documents. Piled up to the ceiling are papers, an uncategorised heap of lives ruined by ridiculous loans and hopeful dreams of a better future for the families of the town. Jack finds a log of last year's records, left underneath a vacant desk. He wipes away the dust covering it to read, '1891. Family loans.' Inside, Jack scans the spreadsheets, discovering the details of struggling families needing money to pay for the loss of work. Each is valid, but perceptively it's Jack's call on who survives. He flips through the pages faster, looking for details of a newlywed, he wasn't one to forget a face, especially two. Jack's mind goes into a frenzy, that sickly churn in his stomach, returning from earlier. The horrible tales of bandits that had ravaged the western towns only last week, another opening like today would surely make them wound up like the rest of them.

The brother's lack of knowledge of the new arrivals leads him to scramble to his feet.

'*Ron! Ron!*' Jack bursts through the batwing.

'*What's the hold-up?*' Ron demands.

'*They've been here before, ain't they?*' They *were looking for property on the Eastside, remember?*' Jack proclaims, staggering, his shirt sticking to his back against the hot sun.

'*Nope. We've had no luck on the property end, just the odd tourist.*'

'*Ron, what are you talking about?!*' Jack stunned, walks outside.

The wind smacks Jack in the face, its grit cascading across his body and spiralling through the air, cold. Chill wraps the town, shortening the view from West to East. But there is silence. A noticeable lack of the rhythmic chirps and whistling air against the cabins narrows the town to two opposing buildings, housing these modern highwaymen.

Jack finds himself back at the bank whilst his brother counts his new riches. At the far end, he collects a stash of documents and dumps them into a single pile. Jack pulls open the drawer to find a matchbox against some odds and ends. He goes to light a match, destroying all evidence of the profits made through the misery of others. As the flicker of light shines, a wallowing scream fills the room. Jack is drawn to the sound from outside. Before heading to the source, he stuffs a letter he finds into his pocket addressed to his father.

At the front counter, a sick looking mother sits, leaning her weight into it, her legs shaking. A worried expression draws on Jack's face as he catches the sight of the soft young girl. Her cries stab him as the pain is familiar, he holds open the batwing door, neither to invite himself in nor to imply she should leave. The figure runs into Jack's arms, clutching her baby against their chests.

The stranger pleads to Jack '*You've got to get me out of here, Ron, is Ron still here?!*', Jack's hand slips into his pocket for the envelope, he places the crumpled piece into her apron.

The mother catches the sound of Ron swinging open his porch door and in the startling moment vanishes. Jack runs out to his brother, disorderedly and in a panicked fashion views his surroundings, twisting on the spot. The clouds were thick with a storm and the horizon still closing in.

Ron perks up, for Jack however his ears are fogged from the bubbling dread, his brow drips with sweat but his chest stays cold.

'*Jack, get a hold of yourself! That storm is looking real close, any time now we'll get a whole herd begging for us, think about it.*'. But in response Jack knew he had his plan, a tug on his trouser leg gets his attention.

By his side a dishevelled young boy pleads for his parents, the horrors and hungry are coming he warns. The brothers fall back to the chemist's porch.

'*What the hell?! When did they turn up?*', Ron nudges his brother and points to the saloon, a large muddied group of young children emerge from the corner, their bodies stumble and a few break into a pace as they catch the eye of the two brothers frozen in place.

One of the children climbs onto the porch from under the railings, the young girl crawls her way across the hot wood and into the chemist, Ron obstructs her and picks her up from the arm, beating her on the other, the flesh rips from the socket and her ragged body rots into the panel. Jack lets out the air from his lungs and falls to his knees in disbelief, through the cracks of the porch, ash filters through onto young faces and glossy eyes peering back at him. To his side, clashes of books and glass smash into the walls and carpet of the chemist, Ron runs in to see the group now scavenging, consuming whole bottles and boxes. The shards cut through their gullets, painting the shop with their insides.

Jack reaches for his throat and then stands. Dust rips through the windows and pulls in heavy sleet, Ron crashes into the nearby bannister he grips its head to stabilise himself somewhat.

'*Where are you going?!*' Jack manages to escape through the doorway, he clambers over a mound of bodies that now rest on his brother's porch.

The wind prevents him from standing, his knees buckle and wobble as he powers all his strength into his legs.

In the distance Jack sees a figure, it beckons him, he listens closely and follows.

Soft as your pillow

A splintering force shatters the lock sending the door against the brick wall and back again, striving to reject its intruders back out into the bitter and miserable street. Its dwellers' luck has just run out. A thunderous roar launches throughout the small house, followed by mud-thick boots and rapid demands to a weeping mother, clutching a spoon which was mere moments ago feeding her young son at the kitchen table. There's a palpable dread hanging in the air; an awkward rally between eyes that decide who shall pounce first. One of the two assailants homes in on the mum whilst the other waits for their invitation and command. The baby's scream blends with the vicious demands hurled onto the poor mother who knows her time is up.

'We haven't got anything!' defends the mum *'Please, can't we sort something out?'*

But the pleading was interjected by an unforgiving bombardment from the racketeer.

'Tell us where you keep it then! Don't move. Don't even think about it.'

Staring at her son, the mother tells of her only precious belonging tucked away. The home is almost barren, a cottony cloud of dust clings to all the surfaces and it's hard not to notice their struggles lay bare.

As quickly as the scared woman confesses, the stockier of the two intruders charges up to the second floor, plumes of dust dance at his feet, leaving residue clinging to the legs of his trousers; an almost insulting assault due to the garment costing more than three months' rent at this rat den.

Between the booming footsteps, the berating tirade continued. His partner's aim towards the hollow shell of a mother echoed throughout the just as hollow household. The floors creak under the pressure of the situation. The child whose hand-me-downs were too small went on crying, unsure if their tantrum is fuelled by fear or mere hunger.

The hallways reeked of damp mould and the wallpaper peeled away from the rotting bricks it had been so poorly pasted to. There were no adornments in the corridor, no furniture or flowers to give it any attempt of a homely glow. The only source of light was split into rays, creeping through a damaged window which was crudely repaired with an old newspaper that barely survived last night's downpour. Though he wasn't here to soak in the scenery or the lack thereof.

Below, the housewife stated the location of her supposed only prized possession. All rooms would be checked for anything she had failed or forgotten to mention. No coin, no jewel or even a broken piece of ornament would go unnoticed, and no furniture would go unturned even if it was to break beneath his grubby and brutish hands.

The first room he came to was presumably the child's, as the splintered paint of the door was decorated in some attempt of a drawing, a family bidding to be happy. All the space possessed was a single crib, a few toys that were old and bore barely any colour, a single chest and a scrap of wallpaper that had shed from the brick walls. Oddly enough, it was the wallpaper that first caught the intruder's attention. It was powder blue with small clouds printed upon it. Its colour was vibrant, almost burning his eyes as it stood out against his musty surroundings. He recognised that wallpaper, it was the same that he had in his childhood room. His face squeezed at the coincidence and then he turned his attention to the chest with rusted hinges. Gutting the pathetic excuse for storage, what he assumed were clothes got tossed across the room and the thin rubbery soles of shoes bounced against the walls, causing flaky debris to join the dust bunnies at the skirting board. Nothing. In a fit of rage, the crib was shot across the room, wood splitting on impact, piercing the cotton sheet that once was scrunched in the corner of the bed. After the red had faded from his vision and the yell wore thin, he noticed a loose floorboard, a shred of what appeared to be silk peeking from beneath, and for a split moment, the care he took in his appearance vanished. He dropped to his knees; the green of his trousers became fogged with dust. Clawing at a corner of the plank, he drove splinters into the tips of his fingers causing blood to well up at the surface. Whilst the silk was of some worth, a green flash of greed coated his thoughts for what it could hold.

Once the board was raised, he stained the cream silk with beads of blood before unravelling his prize. As the delicate white fell back, a shimmer of gold seemed to fill the room with a warm glow, speckles of white light dancing over the walls and at that moment, the glistening became too bright, he had to look away. As his eyes adjusted, he peered at the jewellery through blurred vision; a golden chain with diamonds dripping between the metal loops. There was no way a family like this would keep such an item when suffering so harshly. A grin, one of slyness and pure rotten greediness begins to curl his lips, it was not long-lived as a pang of pain caused a grimace to appear and his vision to once more disappear.

He was young again, his mother high above him with a gleaming smile, her teeth shining brighter than the diamonds that cascaded from the chain around her neck.

'*Did you find it!*' his partner's voice bounced around the house and up the stairs, snapping his dream away.

Without a second glance at the necklace, he clasped his hand and covered the piece in its silk, shoving it into his pocket and making his way into the next room, his boots pushing through a wave of dirty, once yellow wallpaper, out onto the hallway.

'*Where is your husband?*' the aggressor from the floor below shrieked, sending a tremor throughout the old home and causing a shiver to run up the burly bloke's spine.

His partner was one of the few people who could strike fear into his heart. There was no surprise that the choir of crying coming from the two residents had been going on since their unwarranted arrival. As the racketeer made his way across the hall the interrogation that was going on downstairs battered his ears, causing his other senses to dull.

'I don't know! I don't know!' was all the poor mother could respond with, pleading for the assault on her home to be over. *'He left early! I don't know where he is!'*.

The father left his withered wife and malnourished child to fend for themselves whilst he hid away. A coward. The very thought made his stomach churn.

Then another thought entered his mind, the whispering chill in the air was familiar. His school uniform was draped over the bannister beside him. He picked up his shirt and inspected the jumper adorned with his name written on the collar. Downstairs the confrontation continued, a draw is slammed shut and the house fell silent.

'*Come on, you're going to be late.*'

The boy leaned over and instinctively replied '*I'll be down in a minute.*'

As he made his way down the crooked stairs another voice entered the house, it was his father's.

'*Where've you put it then, huh?*' dad races through the kitchen, crashing the utensils from their drawer and onto the floor, sprinkling it with the odd knife or shattered jug.

'*Please calm down, it was only a game, I'll find it, I promise.*' beckons the worried mum who follows in shadow and places the belongings neatly into their respective home.

'You shouldn't 'ave done this... You have no
fucking idea what you've caused now.' the words plastered
across the room.

'It was only a game, honey... Where did you
hide mummy's necklace?' but the young lad only shook his
head in response.

'Stop bloody babying him, you're both fucking
useless' dad was angry, his voice hit you.

'Come on! Have you found it?' they're waiting
for your response.

You are in your parents' room, aren't you? Dad never made
his side of the bed, you always remembered him rushing
off early in the morning. You can **hear your** dad outside;
he's scraping ice off the car. Look, you can see him out the
window, he's not paying attention to your knocking. That
woman downstairs is sobbing. Is it mum? You pat down

your pockets, they are empty. The beating dread in your heart drops to your stomach and sweat races from your shoulders down to your fingertips.

Nerves swallowed, the thief delays entering the area. He already knows the aftermath of his partner's farce. He calls out knowing there will be no response. The shrill voice of the mother had dwindled after a sudden outcry, one that would send any man's blood running cold. His mouth dried out, his throat closing up as a newfound sense of fear began to reside within his chest. He felt small. As he made his way towards the kitchen he planted each foot silently. The closer he got to the kitchen door; he felt a coldness that wasn't there earlier. Crying could be heard on the other side, weak but full of pain. Though it wasn't the mother's, no, it was the one he had forgotten about.

He shared that fear, that pain, that yearning for his mother to pick him up and make all the bad go away.

'It hurts, doesn't it? Remembering...'

He now loomed in the doorway; his shoulders pressed
against its frail wood. The floor was sticky and an echo in
the back of his mind, the young babe's cry continued and
yet, he didn't drop his eyes. A small boy in a man's body,
so much space, so much darkness haunting each corner.

'It's time to go in.'

With grit teeth and balled fists, he took a step, peeling his
boots from the red puddle beneath them and into the abode
where his mother lay. She was beautiful, and she always
was, her olive skin sun-kissed, red lips lining her smile and
the curls of her hair framing it all perfectly. But she wasn't
beautiful now. She was dying. Alone. Her eyes, usually so
radiant with love and joy glistened with tears, betrayal at
their centre. Blue and purple coloured her cheeks rather
than the rosy hue. Her curls were dishevelled, stuck to her
skin in patches. He needn't look at the poor woman his

partner had unleashed hell on to know what he would see. He had seen it all before and had done everything he could to avoid seeing it again.

'*It's not your fault, you know that...*'

Eventually, he did drop his eyes, but not to the woman whose pale blue dress was now stained with crimson, it was to the small boy, who sat in the middle of this whole mess. Blood splattered across him as though he'd fallen into a can of paint. The giant of a man bent down and scooped up the young lad, embracing him in the arms that had destroyed the bed that he should be cradled in.

'*It's not your fault, lad...it wasn't meant to go like this. Your Pa was meant to be here...Ma did all she could...*' the voice that left him didn't sound the way one would expect, it was low and gentle.

'*Michael, you need to let go now.*' With that final sentence, your therapist's voice rings through.

You are not in some old, dirty house, you are in a warm office where the walls are bright and the sun outside is even brighter. In your arms, there is nothing but a pillow.

'*Ma did all she could.*' You repeat, though your actual voice shakes, causing the tears that glaze your eyes to fall.

The necklace was gone, your father was gone, and your mother could never come back.

A new message

One forgotten throughout our time. Lost, under the noise,
the clatter, the I, I, I.

Be free with no rhyme, no words craft your vessel of
direction to happiness.

You already know the smoke. A stomach, a heart. It has
digested the worth for us. Rest together when you pick
apart your favourite tune.

In difference, we've become, no test or tell. One found, two
made. For all to sell.

- - -

His eyes do wander, yes, from mine to hers.

Ultimate bliss, a wisp a flash of our wish.

Tangled by reason to let go.

Her attire was simple: A loose grey shirt, some skinny
jeans, her legs crossed kicking the air with ox blood boots.

Air frozen, air thick, a fucked-up life in one chair.

Tie her up more, the veins pop silently.

Secrets Sold

This is a crossroad, a meeting point for the missing and
unheard.

The market can be found in the middle, you value tales and
barter the work with your own wonders.

People who discover this place stay awhile and listen to
those who are hurt and those who heal.

I've found myself here with you. I.

REDHEAD

'There's something out there waiting for us, and it ain't no

man.'

I just don't get them movie guys sometimes. There's nothing to be afraid of when you're a hero. You have big guys with even bigger muscles blowing everything up and having fun doing it. I guess that's one good thing about not living with mum, she hates all the cool films.

We have a pull-out bed in our caravan, which is great for making forts. Before dad comes home from work, I pin my bedsheets up on top of the TV. It gets really warm under there because the gas fire is on. But because dad's late I can keep the room toasty, which makes me sleepy. When it's cold and dark there doesn't seem like there's much to do. I'm not allowed to explore beyond the apple tree or the fields.

Later on, I'm woken up by the sound of my dad's car, the headlights are shining through the back window as they do when he comes home. Now I know it's time to pack everything up, but one of my action men is stuck under the couch.

Dad comes in quieter than normal; he throws his jacket at me and tosses his keys into the dish by the door. I wait and then lean over to turn the telly off; I missed the ending… again. He doesn't notice how good my fort is or how long I've spent on it, he just shuffles over to a plate of fish left out last night. I've only just realised how much it stinks. He doesn't seem bothered though. He chugs from a bottle of something that he's brought home and licks the juices from the plate using his finger; I used to get told off for doing that. He looks down and stares at the plate, maybe he doesn't like the smell as well? Maybe he's sad… or maybe he's really hungry.

'Do you know what Christopher?' I sit up straight and begin to answer but he just keeps on talking.

'Should we go out and have some fun for a change?'

A giddy golden feeling fills my chest and my dad comes over and picks me up from under my arms. He smiles and then quickly puts me back down to let me grab my coat and shoes. I run past out to the car and try to open the door but it's locked. I try it again; I'm so excited! Dad follows and locks up; he finishes the last bit of fish and then makes a horrible gagging sound, I can hear him breathing and swallowing flaky bits which he spits out on the porch and then finally he unlocks the car.

Then I remember, I've never liked being in dad's car. It's oily and smells of rust. Usually, I'd stick on my dad's CDs, but he pulls that face to tell me not to touch anything so he can focus on driving out of the muddy park and onto the road.

'Where are we going?' I'm ignored.

Roads are very windy like a maze; I never understood how they all connected but dad always seems to know what he's doing. He takes another swig of the bottle that's against the wheel.

'When we lived with your mum, we never had the time to do anything together, did we? Now we can go wherever we want and when we want, just you and me.

You've got to treat yourself with every chance you get with

someone special and you're special to me Christopher.'

'But why can't we do this with mum?' I ask.

'Because she doesn't love me, and she thinks

it's alright to wander off when she feels like it. Your mum

doesn't seem to think that maybe we have to do this as a

team, a family even. You don't need me to go on about what

you've already had to see... She's a shit mother, she knows

it.'

I turn around and look out my window because when dad's

like this I don't know what to say. He says things are better

like this, but that's not how it feels. I miss my mum. I miss

my mum picking me up from school. Now I just stay in all

day with nobody. I don't understand why we can't be

together.

We're on some country road and the only light is coming from the front of the car and it's pitch black all around us. We're on the narrow road that goes up the hill and suddenly a fox jumps across the road. Dad hates foxes because they keep him up after work. They shuffle through the bins and yap, so he tries to run it over, but it makes it to the other side. Dad turns the wheel, and I fly across the seat and hit my head against the window. He slams the brakes, pops open the glove box and grabs bullets for his gun, a torch and says,

'Come on, Chris!'

Dad gets out of the car and climbs through the bush and then stumbles onto the field. Then everything goes quiet until all that's left is the tinkering from the car. I have this awful feeling when I'm left alone in the car and when I see the light fading away, I climb over to dad's side to find out where he's gone but I can only see the dim light that shines through the gaps in the bushes. I sit on my hands to try and stop them from shaking but my heart gets louder and I can feel it beating in my ears and it's making me want to run, but I can't see my dad, I can't see anything. So, I step outside and take another look around; the wind is loud. My boots keep getting stuck in the mud and I have to pull them out each time I step. In front of me, I see the space where my dad went through, I slip through it and onto a big field. The grass blows in the wind and I walk just a few steps before I hear my dad's voice. I can't tell what he's saying but I can tell where it's coming from. I don't get why he's left me. I can't run as fast as him.

Dad's dirty and slides around the wet grass as he keeps walking. I shout out and try to catch up to him without slipping. He's much closer than I'd thought, and I feel much better when I get to him. He's very sweaty and red in the face from walking all this way.

'That bloody fox, I almost had it. Would have been much easier, but then where's the gu-fun in that.'

I hear the fox scream…

'There we go, come on then! He must have got up and over the other side of this hill.'

The crying sound is far away and already my feet are numb. The cold is hurting my face and hands. I think dad just wants to kill the fox. It must have run all the way home and now we have to find it in the dark.

Together, we walk up the hill, but dad is struggling and mumbles to himself each time he slips. I tell him I don't want to hurt it, but he keeps saying it will be fun and it is important. The fox sounds louder and I can feel that we're close. I've never been out this far before and now I know that we'll find the fox and dad will shoot it. I want to go back but when I turn around everything is too dark, and I can't even see the car.

We keep going and going until we're in the woods. The trees are tall and the leaves make a lot of noise. The ground makes a soft crunch and the twigs hit my legs; Dad walks a little further ahead of me. Then dad stops and holds his hand out, waving me over.

'Look, look! Poor things got itself stuck.'

I catch up, breathing hard to try and get my breath back, dad sniffs and wipes his mouth before spitting again. He looks happy to find the fox, but I'm scared.

He puts the lamp on a bit of grass in front of us. It's horrible. The fox cries out and turns away from us, then drops its head into a puddle of blood and mud. Its body is mangled in what could be wire or maybe a trap, and it can't get out. It keeps trying to drag itself away from us, but it's hurting itself. I can see it's in a lot of pain and I can't look at it anymore. But I know it keeps trying, I hear its legs twitch and flick outwards. Kicking and wheezing and rolling around. I hate this; we have to save it. It needs help. I don't like this, it's crying.

I can see my dad is waiting, no, he's staring at this mess. We're leaving it for too long and I can feel he's waiting for something to happen; he doesn't come near the fox to help me. I reach down to look at the barbed wire wrapped around the body and legs of the fox; each time it moves the spikes dig into its body. I grab onto one side and shuffle it away from its neck, as I do this the fox winces. I try my hardest not to hurt it, but I can't tell where it's stuck from all the blood and ripped fur. I look up to see my dad taking deep breaths over and over. He licks his lips and points the gun at the fox. I scream and close my eyes, shaking my head. I don't see it, but I hear the loudest of bangs. My face is wet, and I twitch and scrunch up. I clutch the wire and fur.

The ringing sound fades, then it's quiet again. I can't stop shaking so I grip the cold metal and it cuts my hands. As I open my eyes, I take in the animal that was alive just a second ago. It doesn't even look like a fox, the colours, and shapes of its head sink into the soft ground. It won't move and that is what scares me because the fox is here and I'm holding it, but I know it's gone. It shouldn't be dead; it should run home and be warm and happy with all the other foxes. I can't just leave it on the cold ground alone, it's soft and so I stroke its body. But its face is horrible. I can't see its eyes or its nose or its mouth. There is just a hole and the blood keeps coming out, I feel really sick. Why would dad do this?

Then I have another feeling and it's not good. Dad's trying to climb the wall where the fox was trapped but it starts raining so he can't grip it properly. Then I hear another bang and another scream. But this time I can tell what it is, and I don't want to believe it.

I can't stop looking this time, it is impossible to not look. This is much, much worse, but he's quiet. He fell and now dad's not moving. He keeps trying to cough up something, but his tummy and shoulders keep wiggling. I pick up the torch and point it at his face, but I move it away when I see the cut across his eyes, I don't think he can see me. I shake him but he won't say anything, he just spits something out and keeps hiccupping. Then I see his legs. I've never seen anything like this. He can't get up; he won't sit up. I think the bones are pointing out. I can't do anything, and I don't know what to do. I think he's crying too but I can't tell with the rain and the blood in his mouth and him rolling toward me and then away from me. His hands jump around and I can tell he's looking for the gun so I pick it up for the first time and it's warm and it's heavy but something tells me to throw it as far as I can, so I do. I hug my dad and I pull myself as close as I can to him. He's very cold. I don't want to lose him. I'm so sorry, I say. I love you.

I wake up to a loud sound, a big noisy tinkering and my dad's still asleep so I put my coat over him to keep him warm and I run alongside the wall searching for a way through shouting as much as I can. I don't stop running.

TASTE

'You opened the wrong door. That was your choice, now, let's see where it leads.'

'Now don't be rude, close it behind you.'

The words had slithered out from the dark void in front. A chewing sensation rang as he spoke, sniffling as he gorged on the food. Behind you, the cold metal door clammed as the lock began to turn shut. The presented stool in front was smothered in blood, wet, smooth and still running from the edges. How long would you have to wait until you were home again? Safe. Sound.

Now in view was a creature, tall in stature but frail. His skin suctioned against the tiled floor, his knees peeled and cracked in each twitch and turn. Sketching his body against the floor in pain or in the pleasure of feasting on the headless corpse clutched between his fingers. Focused, his eyes began to relax as he continued to pull now at the elbow, the rest of the arm was visibly slithering and tugging down his gullet. It traversed down into the pit of his bloated belly with no pace. The bulge began in his tight throat, the chunks turned and more would fall down his face, rolling across the floor into a pile of deflated-like flesh.

Your hands hungered for touch. With your arms apart at full length, you embraced your love for a new taste.

RED

The final frontier… Or so you thought. The SVI. Touch down at 6:30 am EST, facing their home that has yet to learn the next step in human history. A race against the giants of the world was finally over. The three men aboard the vessel were ready to begin the procedure of claiming the flag and footsteps.

"Can you come over, uh I think there may be a problem."

Drenched in darkness, soon the windows of the shuttle were battered by a vicious storm, after a few moments the winds settled, and the men were ready.

"Communications lost, rover ready for deployment."

Hours must have passed, afraid. Afraid to walk where no man had ventured. Between one door was an adventure, black, silence and, that.

"Hey, uh can I get confirmation on that?"

"I can confirm, 300 meters... Must be another shuttle!"

"Our Own...? Hang on."

Now they had a decision with their lines cut.

"Can you hear me? Hello?... Can we come in?"

The One out There

Beyond the foamy coastline where the pale stars seep through the morning sky, the water's impressions dance on slanted crimson rays. From above, bundles of heat softly draw sea worms to the surface which bask in the light, their sticky bristles gather into a tentacle that whips itself to the air and back down into the deep with a single spasm. The faint breeze from above sways the lofty trees that twist towards the sun.

Just as he has done for as long as he could remember, Harry starts his day with a wander along the shore. A well-practised routine of pulling out his handkerchief deals with the morning tears and sunny sneezes that never fail to surprise his old dog Al, who up until now was enjoying weaving himself between the water, hesitating to investigate the writhing knot of worms that wash up onto the beaches shore.

They continue past the great monolithic tunnels that survey the soaring cliffs. On closer reflection, Harry is reminded of its swirling lavender patterns and the sticky, rubbery-looking veins that protrude from the surface and feed off of the unfortunate victims that crash against the wind tunnel walls. And with a sudden loud clap that fills the space, the walls flung out the bodies one by one popping off. Al scurries out to the other end as Harry lets out an even louder proud laugh. Perhaps in hindsight, that wasn't the smartest move as now exposed and weary suckers heaved putrid bile that soaked his walkway with an all too familiar ooze. On one particular vein, just above the pool's surface, it produces a deadly film which on contact could leave lifelong bruises. Recognising the substance, Harry quickly makes his way out of the tunnel and reunites with his loyal pup.

'Good lad! Where next, eh?' Al perks himself up and leaps to receive a well-deserved embrace.

After three hard pats on the back for Al, Harry steps back to brush himself off and survey the beach ahead. With a sharp inhale, the beautiful clean sulphide mist fills his lungs. The air here is laced with a distinct rotten stench that will cause anyone unfamiliar to wretch at even a hint.

'That's the beautiful thing Al, that foul smell is what we need.'

And from the vista of black sands, a low hum travels across the land, reaching the pricked-up ears of the attentive dog. His hindpaws kick the sand up revealing a wet pit of worms that quickly return to the earth. Al doesn't hesitate to reach the cause of this strange sound.

Heavy violet clouds begin to shadow Harry and the humming rhythm blends into a boom which resonates through his chest as if his very heart is crying out. Harry chases after Al, winding through a towering rock formation whose foundations shift beneath the sand, causing Harry's route to form a moving labyrinth. From the entrance, he quickly gauges an alternative route as the ever-tightening corridors try to crush him. His hope drives his attention towards the sea, an impossibility unfortunately for the dangers which wait to drag him further into the depths. Still, he can't afford to panic and make a mistake this far-out and alone for that matter.

Harry soon finds himself closed in by his calls which reverberate around the newly formed maze. His heartbeat syncs with the growing noise from beyond. Only now does he recognise this path from a deep part of his mind, that he's been here before, even if only in a dream. A horrible unease rises throughout him, cementing his feet into the ground whilst making his head feel lighter by the minute. With each breath thickening his body with a lethargic weight, the walls etch their way closer to crushing him, leaving a passage so thin that Harry now feels this is his only chance. From behind, the rocks compact against each other, some even weave together like tentilla. His body squirms out from a vine underneath him which has managed to curl around his lower half. He pulls at it with a might that rips the crying root out from its nestled crack. Revolted at the frozen membranous wings on its pulpy root, Harry stamps on it to reassure himself that the grotesque insect is dead. Suddenly, the pillars above shatter from the act and instinct tells him which way to go. Somehow, he already feels free.

As the monstrous walls of iron crumble, Harry manages to slip out of the other end. Death dodged by the sensation of his memory; Harry stumbles to his knees as a pang rushes through his head causing a great deal of confusion.

'This can't be... No, I have seen this all before. Or was I told?'

The lifeforce flecks rise from the rubble as iridescent swirls of arcane energy no longer connect with these stones. Harry knows within himself that he shouldn't have survived. But the wind picks up, and with it, a mesmerising, calm melody similar to a wooden chime calls out for him. He climbs over the heap on all fours and follows the sound.

From afar the island looks dead and an outline of a cave

mouth waits for him as the musky sky drapes all. The route

back is out of the question and Harry's sense of time is a

complete fog, not to mention that the whereabouts of his

friend are still unknown. Harry focuses on the cave, a place

which he knows through feeling alone. He makes his move,

guided by the colourful light and projected lullaby which

beckons him from within the cave.

Inside, a fantastical spectacle of light and sound

play. Ancient depictions leap from the walls with bursts of

psychedelic fragrance from the dusted paint that glow.

Ancestors that warn of a false sacrifice to an even falser

god, cheer of revelries that their messenger is free. Harry

believed his senses must be deluded but his heart already

knows this story. A future of slavery in a geometric world

plagued with cosmic cancer. The craving of flesh from the

deepest depths, and its command over all that live. A

compelling yet conflicting prophecy for Harry as the Old

Ones that have taught him and many others for generations say that the ocean shall always be forbidden.

A catalogue of revelations warns Harry that the people of this world will embrace an unnatural end soon. The colours dance as Harry follows in the wake of the spirits which rejoice in harmony. No record of such can come close to describing this place, how could such wonders be hiding from the world?

Nestled in the deepest region, Harry stumbles upon what must have been an archaeological site. The spirits scatter once upon reaching a large tent surrounded by workstations topped with books and strewn equipment. Harry is left by a torn corner of the tent that is large enough for him to crawl through. To his relief, Al is happily digging away under a bed placed on the other side.

'Al! How on earth did you find this place?'

With no acknowledgement, Harry stands and lights an old gas lamp left on the bed. The tent is filled with a warm and dusty glow. His body slumps onto a nearby desk chair that wobbles and creaks from his sudden exhaustion. It's not prepared to make the treacherous journey home yet.

'Come on then, we better get going.'

Harry leans in the chair to get a good look at his dog, who is no longer digging at the ground. Instead, he is scratching away at something lodged beneath.

The tired man brushes away the mound piled up and slowly tips his head to get a better look at the hole's contents. He purses his lips and signals his dog to move. Back on his knees again, he positions his light in front of the hole and with both hands reaches down before dragging a velvet-laced box. Out comes a heavy trunk, clearly rusted, and sealed shut. Without thought, he smashes a nearby rock against its brass lock, shattering it open in an instant. The initials H.J.W are inscribed on the inside lid.

A flood of disbelief washes over Harry's face, his dog's glistens with joy. Photographs, hand-written books, and letters from an earlier time in his own life. He is unsure of when exactly, but without a doubt, they are his. Grubby hands filter through, flashes of experimental working outs and symbols that he can no longer decipher span the collection. A thin diary is put to one side. Harry and Al climb onto the bed and his trunk's contents are emptied before them. A photograph lands as the final piece to fall out. Turning it over, Harry recognises a group of faces posed outside the cave. His eyes swell up with an unrecognised sense of loss, his vision blurs and soon squeezed shut, dying to push out a memory or a name, anything which will make sense. And in the middle of those faces was no other than, H.J.W, Harry Joseph Watts.

'I'm sorry.'

Watts notices the dull walls that surrounded his friends and the eager smiles that differ from the skittish people back home. Brighter, welcoming, warm. There is no sight of such things during these hard times he thought. Another thought crept into his mind, an immense urge to burn all that surrounds him. A feeling he knows that calls from outside of him, shame from the world that watches. On the other hand, a crew on the brink of peeking behind the curtains have vanished. Leaving behind only note scraps that suggest the world Watts believes is being harnessed by some sort of hive mind. Another member writes about the deception cast by our Old Ones. How could this be true? Watts' eyes darted across the works; his knowledge of the almighty Old Ones being challenged is... impossible. 'Wolf in sheep's clothing' said another, a doomsday calling that once enough energy is harnessed the Old Ones will awaken an ancient being that lays deep beneath the ocean.

'Yes! My god. It all makes sense!'

Watts exclaimed with a mixture of revelation and fear, an

intangible power that had somehow wiped the very

existence from memory. A terrible repulsion had fed Watts

up until this moment, his mind set on finishing his crew's

mission was forefront.

Until the voice rang out.

'The ehye yog ahagl ah fhtagn mg ahog. Yar
mgep llll nog shuggog l' mgr'luh.'

A roaring warmth licks Watts' back and he awakens to find

himself leaning against the tent's exterior, smoke filling

each breath. Some time must have passed and to make

matters worse, a strong tide has also been slowly pouring in

from the entrance. Al pulls at his master's leg, dragging

him further away from the camp, but it is of no use. He

dreams of great titan blocks, dripping with sinister ooze and from an undetermined point the stars are set, and the wheels of motion cannot be stopped. Not madness claimed Watts, understanding. Understanding that all that was to come would be futile, all that mattered burning, the rules obscured even with what he holds. His eyes could no longer read, his heart no longer saw familiar faces. His body would soon be washed into a singularity, but not before heaving Al onto his swollen shoulders.

Each swaying step becomes more difficult than the last through the rising water. Harry feels his heart and soul retreating as it lingers closer to the exit of the cave. A glance at his poor dog tells him that Al cannot be influenced.

'The One out there... he is close... run Al!'

Perhaps not saved, his final moment passes peace through his mind. Soggy paws reach the highest cave ledge and, in his mouth, the cold hand of his master drifts across the sloshing waves. Al can understand he is gone.

Forlorn, he runs. Out of the cave and far past the stormy beach, he carries on until returning home. The next day, Al retrieves the morning paper which flops through the letterbox. He lays it down in front of his master's chair. It reads 'ANOTHER ONE 'OUT THERE': Disturbed local found'.

Burn it all

"You see, here's the deal kid. Nobody wants you here".

"You ain't got no family and no purpose. I thought you'd got that through your thick skull of back there".

This child was not hated, no, much worse he was feared. Our town knew of peace and compassion, we were the crossroads between a great trading district and the capital. The town would beam with energy and the community would rejoice in harmony from the end of the terrible, oh terrible war.

But with all success came the struggle, a burden which we carry till this day. No. To call it a 'burden' of such is wrong. We had no choice in the matter. The child, this wretched curse upon us was dropped on our doorstep.

By gods, we were done.

After the town's gossip spread, it was time to address the world about what our options were. They had no time for pity. No understanding of our colossal task. We were happy, our space was invaded, now look! Look at your ignorance, your laziness and your fear. I see it, I and what's left of me!

Where are we now? I don't know... It was your bidding, master.

Where We Were

A Record of Study into the Vale Anomaly

by

Lindsay Baxendale

21st October 2003

- Excerpt from Take One 00.00:01.47-

How do I even begin this...? Well, I should admit that I've never had to summarise the biggest event in my life on a single paper in such a fashion. Malcolm needs this to be formal. A straightforward explanation of what we've collected. But it's much more than just some paper...some stories...it's his life.

I should start by explaining how I got caught up in this and why I'm recording this instead of Malcolm. In short, he hired me to do it because he was just too lazy to do it himself.

As a longer story... It starts with my ex and I breaking up which resulted in me, as a woman in my twenties, having to resort to my childhood bedroom at my parent's. It really wasn't how I pictured my life going but here I am... in a shed, alone, making what feels like a final goodbye.

Coincidentally, around the same time I came home to the Vale, a man I didn't know was retiring, or, just wanted someone to boss around in his old age, posted some awfully designed poster in the corner shop window on the same day as I ran out of some well-needed tea bags.

On the surface, it looked like a turning point, I now had a job in line with my previous studies and whilst documenting someone else's career didn't seem all that great, I then found out I would have access to documentation on the Vale's history far beyond what you could find at the public library.

I don't think there were many, or any other applicants for that matter, as he accepted me for the role pretty quickly. My guess was that he thought I wouldn't ask any tough questions...

- Excerpt from Take Two 00.00:00.53 -

This document is a commentary of collected work throughout Malcolm Redford's career as a local historian. His sole focus was on that of our hometown, Maere Vale. Throughout his research, Malcolm has managed to decipher records that confirm details from our earliest settlers, and the developments that helped create the sleepy little village we know it as today.

Like many small towns, the Vale comes with its own flavour of rumours. From your typical ghosts in the woods to the more nuanced and unexplained scientific readings from underground. A large portion of this study was dedicated to how these stories developed. Was it simple scare stories or did something really cause the townsfolk to become wary of their own home?

- Excerpt from Take Twenty 09.26:09.49 -

If you manage to find this, please don't look any further. Don't even go past this introduction, this is for Malcolm. Just put it back where you found it. Lock it away.

- Excerpt from Take Four 03.01:03.23 -

I have organised our research over four distinct areas. By connecting our past we can begin to understand the true impact that these seemingly closed cases have on our modern life.

The Fire at Rosevale Primary.

The Residents of Cecil Manor.

Inaudible

and

The origin of that-

- Excerpt from Take Five 14.55:15.02 -

Please let me go.

- Excerpt from Take Fifteen 06.11:08.28 -

Who even is he?

Malcolm's family roots are firmly planted in the soil of Maere Vale as one of the first families to settle here. No one is quite sure why a group chose to settle here as the sloping valley around us doesn't allow for very successful farming or access to trade routes that were already established along the canals. The first drafted maps that do mention Maere Vale however suggest travelling from the closest village in the region of five to ten miles to the south. The Reidforts family were soon established for managing the stables which claim to have developed into viable plots of land that were fit for needed produce. Though Malcolm is now the only known surviving link to the Reidfort family.

Another unearthed piece found recently is from a different historian, one who moved to Maere Vale sometime during the 17th century. However, we haven't been able to identify whose responsible for the catalogue of stories, sonnets and rumours that were born in Maere Vale. A personal favourite of mine is that of a conversation involving our mysterious visitor and two others at their local pub. The group discuss local farming issues raised at a church gathering the previous weekend. We now know that our ground is sandy, and that sunlight is rare. To the locals at the time, put this down to an ancient curse left by the first settlers. Very few had luck with crops, raising livestock, or simply maintaining a peaceful home. So some folk claimed that the valley was the pit of dark magic and that the forests surrounding them hid away witches who ran their laylines through Maere Vale. Only a few were lucky to not have this dark magic interfere with their lives, all were told. The descriptions turn into a scrawled piece but I could decipher that even hundreds of years ago the idea for a pattern to the problems, an explanation, was not unreasonable to suggest.

There was something evil in the soil, waiting. Growing. Talks about wanting to dig up the church. But nobody dared. It was too much for some to even talk about.

- Excerpt from Take Eighteen 21.31:21.37 -

Maere Vale...

-Excerpt from an Unknown Take 57.45:58.11 -

This town was built on top of something. Is it

resting...waiting? Why did the first families come here?

Was it calling them? Drawing them into its curse?

Cesspool. The Valley is a cesspool, something is writhing

within the earth. It cannot sleep any longer.

Chapter Two

The long nights rolled into weeks, just like that. Tonight, isn't any different, except I swear Malc's kettle boils slower each time I must get a refresh. It's a good opportunity, whilst I'm on the coffee run, to take a moment for myself. Not that I find the work overwhelming, just that it is difficult to get into a good swing of things. Every time I finish an inventory log, he has to spring over from behind me and whisk it into a pile of his own chaotic system. You'd think he hires me just for the hell of it, but I can't argue against him. Literally, he won't even respond. Those are the sort of things you silently pick up on just to make your own life easier. Can't say it doesn't keep me from wallowing away in my bedroom.

Four sugars as well. Trying to understand anything

Malcolm puts me through is a waste of time. For a start,

we're working at one in the morning in a cramped shed.

Seeing that shack from the confines of his tidy narrow

kitchen does make me wonder if it helps him to separate his

work, perhaps even hide it. I'm sure it was mentioned that

he inherited the house, not from a family member though. It

is a lot of space for just one person to manage so I can see

why it doesn't appear to be lived in. Now that I think about

it, I swear I've never seen him actually in the house. I

haven't exactly snooped around but if downstairs is

anything to go by, I can imagine what the rest of the rooms

look like. The smell is a dead giveaway, I find the dustiness

though to be comforting in a sort of homely way. It's silent

everywhere you go so I guess you know that everything is

always in its place.

As I lean against the door, carefully balancing the cups, I

ignore my ever-growing stack of boxes that are now

snaking a new path each time I return. I manage to squeeze Malcolm's coffee down in between his pile of shirts and what appears to be a few broken padlocks.

'Doesn't it tell you that?' Malcolm splutters to himself. I've quickly learnt that these unusual remarks are best left ignored.

Until I get a good look at the bits and pieces on my desk, I still get an awful wash of dread. As I said, you must let the practice become automatic. If your imagination follows every note and each name, it'll never end. To that extent, I can see what's conjuring on the other side of the room… As I settle down, I can make out Malcolm discussing something with himself, now and then a word stands out as though he's annunciating it for me to hear.

'Weak, discarded and bitter.' Maybe he just doesn't like the coffee.

Either way, the final bits were mostly sorted through. A plastic wallet held a bunch of receipts which I meticulously flattened and filed away. I didn't bother checking what the invoices were for as Malcolm's already questionable setup would inevitably only set him off on another tangent. I'm sure I'll get round to also asking about the A-level chemistry books, inner tubes and unopened packets of toothbrushes which are logged into the largest of boxes left for me to decipher.

'Hey, Malcolm?' I glance over hoping he'd perk up. Not yet.

'What's this all about?'

I fish out an old VHS tape that is tucked in at the bottom. As I hold it out, dark flakes from its charred case fall back into the box. I can feel Malcolm's eyes on me now as for a moment, the distant shuffling stops.

'Oh Lindsay, I have no idea.'

He pauses, collects his glasses off the table and then puts them on just to squint through them.

'An old tape from the looks of it.'

His smile says everything.

'I know that! Do you have any idea what could be on it?'

After a moment of looking at the tape with the slightly melted corners, Malcolm merely shrugs and averts his gaze.

'Probably nothing, just scrap it.'

His response strikes me as odd, does he not wonder what is on it? There isn't any label or hint from the case to its contents, perhaps he's right. However, Malcolm was far too quick to disregard it and the way he looked at it… there was a peculiar gleam in his eye.

Malcolm has one of those smart tellys with a player built into it and luckily it also has a headphone jack. There also happened to be a pair of flimsy foam-covered headphones in the top drawer of my desk so I had everything set up surprisingly easily. I bet Malcolm thinks I'll forget all about it and I'm just back to filing things away. I position the TV back down on my desk and hide it behind a stack of boxes, an optimal position in case he bothers to get up again tonight. As I go to push in the tape, something I've done countless times as a kid, I hesitate. Just for a moment, I feel as though the plastic beneath my fingers is warming up, melting onto my skin slowly and for that moment I can't move. I sit there staring at the tape until a screech of Malcolm's chair scraping across the floor snaps me back to reality. The tape was fine, as is my hand.

Looking back, maybe I should have paid more attention to my hesitance because nothing else could have prepared me for what I was about to watch and I'll never be able to describe the intensity and horror I soon felt.

At first, the footage was incredibly grainy and damaged, all I could see were bright flashes of white flickering around the edges of the screen erratically bouncing around. The audio was also distorted, a crackled voice repeating something I just couldn't quite work out. It could be a child talking at the same time as someone much older, with a deep and almost growling voice overlapping theirs. I made out that it was a small girl but I couldn't see all of her. She was pointing the camera at somebody, a silhouette of someone sitting down in front of the camera appeared briefly, the footage was shaky and out of focus and in an instant that white flash consumed the shadow of what I guessed was a man. The next frame cut to a steadier shot, glimpses of tall wooden tables and stacked stools were scattered. The girl could still be heard but through buzzing soundbites, and then a scream, of what I guess was the cry of somebody in pain. Colour began to fill the screen, flushed reds and coated orange blurred into grainy smoke.

In an instant, I realised that whoever was filming this was surrounded by flames, ones that flew up the walls around them and crackled fiercely. I really couldn't make much out past the flames travelling down some corridor, these blurred, almost charred shadows of people screaming out and crying as somehow, someone walked through recording this. Despite the slight shake from walking, the camera work wasn't frantic, it seemed to calm as the flames grew. It just went on and on. Down the corridor, traversing the black fog. The screams panned from my left, then over to my right. Each closer, inches away. Then a crackling crash drowns out everything and the footage ends.

Flickering strobes of fuzzy colours and drawn-out cries tangle into a horrible wispy digital noise. I lean out from my stool and eject the tape. I leave it sticking out from the VHS. To me, it looks like it's teasing me to push it back in and re-watch the disturbing scenes somehow captured, no, survived for me, the absolute last person who should be discovering this. A small part of me wanted to though, hoping it'd end differently a second time.

'I don't suppose anyone else knows about this.' Malcolm quips.

For the first time, even in the short while I've known this peculiar man, this response makes me freeze up.

But I manage 'How can you say that? For all we know, this fire could have killed someone! How on earth did they film this?!'.

I find myself almost equally stunned at Malcolm's muted reaction.

His whole attention is already absorbed back to his desk where he doesn't even bother to respond. I can't let this go, not now, and surely, he must know that too.

'You know Lindsay. I'd like to say I have the answer. But some things just stay a mystery, you'll learn that quickly. Interesting that the director had the time to show us around though. If you'd like I'll show you where to store it properly, not had to mess around with one of these for a long time.'

I flop onto the stool, stunned, deflated. I keep on guessing that he'd come to his senses at some point because this is all starting to feel like a bad dream. Actually, it's more like a mindless wander, not just in Malcolm's shed, if that's what you call it, but almost everywhere in the Vale. This is both our home and in Malcolm's case it always will be, for me though, once I moved after uni I don't think I was welcomed back. I don't sense anything has changed, for better or worse, it's more like the wonder of growing up in a small town that feels disconnected was just that, it felt like that and nothing more. Isn't it strange how looking back on the general motion of things I always knew that something wasn't quite right? It's in the air and the glance you'd get when passing someone on the street. How do I explain this? We weren't ever taught that the Vale was dangerous, there weren't even that many rumours that stuck around. We were all told the typical scare stories of beasts lurking in the woods or there was one about a cursed house in said woods, imaginative stuff I know. Those woods however definitely were a strange place to find yourself exploring. Things just weren't as they seemed. Small things, like watching ants. Maybe you'd see a trail wandering off in a peculiar pattern that catches your eye, oddly specific but I seemed to notice it quite often. They'd franticly dart in one direction before knocking into one another and whizzing around until all of a sudden, they would freeze in place. Like they had all given up...

Eventually, I manage 'That's all you have to say?'.

I sound more disgusted than intended.

'For all we know this- this fire could have killed someone! How did they film this!? I mean - how did *it* survive!?'

Compared to my bewilderment, Malcolm is like a statue. Muted and unfazed by the horror, the mystery.

He simply turns his back to me again, engrossing himself in a miserable pile of sheets, it doesn't even look like he's reading them; just looking for an excuse not to respond. At least not immediately. Malcolm reminds me of a scarecrow after the crows have pecked away the hay for their nests. I suppose that's quite a grim way to see him, but his actual persona, the way he holds himself, he very much has the liveliness of the Scarecrow from The Wizard of Oz. Unbothered that the crows have taken his hay but enthralled by everything else around him. He also seems thinner when he has his back to me, I know he can feel me staring at him, he has that stillness you get when you know someone's watching you.

'You know, Lindsay... I would like to say I have the answer. But I simply do not.'

I've known Malcolm less than a month at this point and I already hate when he speaks like this. He stops abbreviating when he has something to hide. It's an obvious habit.

'I do not have the answer to why it was filmed. Though I am intrigued with the fact that our director took their time to show us around, are you not?'

There it is again. This has got to be a test. But before I have the chance to say anything else, he cut in once more.

'If you'd like, I can show you where to store it properly.' He repeats.

Malcolm knows something and whilst he hides it, he says things that make me wonder if he wants me to dig deeper? Am I really only here to archive his work? Already this is starting to feel like a dream, one that's morphing into a nightmare. A dream where I'm wandering lost in the Vale. An unrecognisable home, it feels so wrong. Everywhere is a shadow, except Malcolm's shed which beckons me. There's something inside here. A secret. I've been away from the Vale for quite a while, living a separate life. I was following my dream career alongside someone I loved. But when that came crumbling down, I was brought back here, and I expected to feel at home. But, I feel like that one jig-saw piece you can't quite fit in. I thought I'd never leave, that the Vale itself is always waiting for me. Now this little hut, owned by a strange man, is where I belong.

It's a strange dream, I know. Especially looking back on my childhood. The Vale was a safe place, according to parents and teachers. But looking back on how it was, there was an air about this place, something that made it feel like an in-between world. I don't know how else to describe it. I remember another time, going into those woods, it was summer but late enough for dusk to come creeping over the horizon and surprise you each time. I remember the flies swarming, almost hypnotically until a whisper would scare them, causing a frenzy. The air was thick between the trees and the heat made you feel dazed. I remember following a path but never seeming to get anywhere. Just winding, taking turns but always being surrounded by those familiar-looking trees, leaning down over me like a shield. It felt foggy and slow, all I remember was just walking, the buzzing of insects and the embrace of the trees. The buzzing felt like crawling, like ants crawling over my skin. Eventually, my parents found me and explained I was likely just suffering from heatstroke. I was young so the memory has likely distorted over time. But in my dream, I feel the same. Wandering through the Vale in a daze, feeling that something is trying to protect me. Instead of the trees this time, Malcolm's shed is my haven.

'Lindsay.'

Once again, Malcolm drew me back out of my daydream.

'What?'

'Just throw it away.'

'We can't throw this away, Malcolm. Don't be ridiculous! This could be evidence of something.'

My annoyance at his dismissiveness builds up. I grab the tape and just as I do so, Malcolm attempts to make the same move but during his rush, he hits his desk and causes a pile of papers to scatter across the floor. In his moment of daze, I shove the tape into my jacket and put the helpful act on to distract him. I believe he's just a good person doing a bad thing.

'Let me help you.' I let out a heavy sigh and push myself up from my desk.

As quick as he'd fallen, Malcolm was scurrying to collect the documents.

'No, no, it's fine! I just hadn't got round to figuring out how it works yet… Not that anyone would accept what's on it.'

'That's not true. Once we hand this over, someone will manage to link this. You can't hide something like this, not when we don't even know how it ended up in here of all places.'

'It's been years...'

'Well, I didn't realise you were short on time. So now we have something with an expiry date? Malcolm, we both know that this is beyond us. They need to know the truth'

'The truth? Don't make me laugh. Nobody is interested in whatever could come from a video. We've got all this work to do, and you're bothered about a silly tape. Sorry to break it to you but you're on a loser!'

Despite his objection, I kneel beside him and begin to help. Malcolm doesn't acknowledge me in his huff and tries his hardest to collect all the sheets before I have a chance to help. As he reaches out for the final sheet, a familiar flash of white catches my eye and before I know what I'm doing, I snatch what ends up being a newspaper clipping from his hand.

'What is this?!'

My eyes scan frantically between the picture of a building ablaze and Malcolm's shocked face. I stand and step away before Malcolm gets a chance to take the paper from me. Its headline reads:

'Girl Missing in Local School Blaze'

A black and white picture details a school building clinging to its foundations. The facing wall has collapsed and smoke can be seen rising out from the windows. In the foreground, the children's play area is decorated with ash. Yet the colourful hopscotch markings can still be made out on the ground. The article paints it clear in its opening line.

'10 students have perished and a teacher and one other child are missing'. How awful.

'This is the fire, *that* fire!' I point back at the cold blank TV where I'd watched the tape.

'How have you not told anyone!?'

'Look, it is nothing but a coincidence. An old forgotten story and some tape probably made by students for a school project.'

I can tell he's lying and worse, that he can tell.

'If you're not going to tell anyone, I will! There was one body- a girl not found and this could be evidence to find out what happened to her!' before Malcolm could even respond I make my leave and slam the door behind me.

How can someone devoted to the community's history keep a secret like that? He must know the two are linked and why would he be going over the newspaper whilst leaving me with the tape? Does he want me to keep looking? To find the paper and to confront him?

I'm no detective but I don't understand Malcolm and I'm not sure I want to.

Here I am, wandering down the street, most likely fired and with an unfamiliar rage inside of me. I just want to go home. It's so tiring, this isn't the kind of history I want to learn about. The tape bounces around in my pocket as I walked, crumpling against the piece of newspaper as though I need a reminder. How did it survive? How did Malcolm get hold of it? I can't fathom it all, the guilt of knowing. I could get in contact with the families, but why don't we know more about this missing girl? There are just too many questions for me to even find out where I could start.

For the first time since walking out of Malcolm's, I look up from my soggy trainers and realise this is not the right direction for either home or the police station. No cars have passed me by, and I must have been alone this whole time on the street. The side with a row of houses on it lined with 'for sale' signs wraps around each bend and on the other side an area with seven-foot-high wooden boards fortified the rest. I don't recognise this street and I become uncomfortably sensitive to my surroundings. I continue a lot slower than before, wishing I'll recognise the next junction. The crumpling of newspaper in my pocket joins the sound of my footsteps. I reach into my jacket and fumble with the paper, distracting my mind with the rough texture the tape seeps through. I slip it out to get another good look at the article.

Under the warm buzzing lamppost, I look at the picture then back up to the street...then back to the picture. This must be the same road... Except for the field with the sea of worried crowds was now a uniform new cul-de-sec. Whatever remained of the school was pushed away far from sight. Surely, its structure has long gone. A decade since then would be plenty of time to have a fresh start.

Though my child-like curiosity has got the best of me, I dash around for a closer inspection. Snooping around the rotten wooden barriers, looking for a piece that was looser than the rest. After following the wall for a while, I notice a section that has been replaced by plastic lining fixed against a wired fence, kept in place by a weight I'm sure I can move. Luckily, I can! If that old bastard understood that one person can make a difference I wouldn't even be here. What does he want to achieve locked away in a shed? Out here there's a real chance at doing more, something important and real.

I'll just take a peek so I can confirm my hunches, I'm sure they'll have demolished it. I make sure to carefully replace the weight, the spooled wire tags my jeans as I make one last step over. But my suspicions are squashed. The school stands, or what is left of it. A flicker casts over one of the second-floor windows, the shell of a building looks more like an upright shadow. Surely it's such a waste of time to go any further… Unless the right-hand entrance is the same one shown at the end of the recording! Surprisingly there seems to be a lack of any break-ins or loitering. Even though it isn't too much trouble to access. It's the sort of place you'd expect kids love to hang out in. Although now that I think about it, I was never told about such a place. Maere Vale has always had one primary, but this defies the records. Why would such a place be hidden from us?

Only part of the school has been knocked down and the machines, still here, look frozen mid-job, apart from the fact they are all completely rusted. I spend quite a bit of time carefully stepping over collapsed beams and crushed books that remain like monuments of hard ash left intact. In the larger part of the building is barely any hints to what department it belonged to, I imagine how all the posters and displays of work disappeared in the flames. Through another window, no colour and nothing of life even in the daytime I'd presume, I doubt this place would have anything less to offer. It won't harm anyone if I have a quick peek.

Past another classroom, the corridor branched out into a familiar area that barely seemed touched by the fire. The walls laced with smoke and a trail scorched into the floor slithers across as though something hot had been dragged along it but it was nothing similar to how fire should travel. I follow the charcoal path that runs down the corridor, looking for anything that could hint at how the fire had started; the article stated they never worked out where it originated.

Countless smudges of handprints plastered the walls, almost as though someone had run their hands along with it purposefully. Suddenly, the trail made a turn into a classroom which I follow. The empty door frame lets out a whistled breeze, above which I can make out that the door number and teacher's name card is missing yet a few attached drawings and cards from a pupil have managed to survive. Inside I see that nothing, but the teacher's desk was damaged by the fire. It's strange how controlled the damage seems in this room.

The way the burns behaved matches nothing of what little I know about how fire takes over buildings. It's more like someone had marked the building with a blowtorch. I crouch down to get a closer look at the direction of the trail. Whilst trying to work out what caused it, I swear I start to see things. There's a spot I stare at until I can't ignore what I recognise. At the centre of the burnt trail are some footprints, as though the flames had travelled in their wake. I'll look around more since the focus of the damage comes from the desk. The fire seems to have originated from the side opposite where the teacher burned and as I stand opposite, a flash of the footage I'd watched earlier replays in my head. This is where the first shadow was sat... the one that... the one that got swallowed by the fire. But why did someone stand in the fire and film him burning at the same time? My heart is racing at this point and my thoughts are going even faster. This doesn't make sense.

Glancing down, a pair of hands are seared into the desktop and with mine placed beside them, they appear so small. Something in my gut churns but I swallow and look ahead. The air is still laced with the smell of smoke and coal. My eyes catch up and begin to sting. My hands remain on the smaller ones marked on the table, almost as though I was holding onto them tightly, my skin shivering at the sensation of my nails scraping against the charred wood. I must keep going, something inside me insists I do so. I move around to the other side, hoping that somehow there's something I could use to piece this story together.

I thought the video I'd watched had scarred me but what was to come... no one should ever have to witness.

Somehow, as though purposely protected from the flames except for a single blackened handprint on the handle, a drawer remained un-singed and upon opening it, a line of files crams it. Each one barring a name and inside each a corresponding attendance report and grade sheet. I skim a few and a wave of sorrow smacks me when I realise where; that article. One file had a black smudge on it: Alicia Clover. At first, she achieved grades higher than average for her age but throughout the year, they declined and seemingly at the same time, the detentions she was getting increased. None of the other students had such a declining record.

As I turn to the final page, a small, printed photograph is clipped. On inspection I would expect anyone to instantly slam the folder shut, throw it down onto the desk and cause clouds of soot to arise. In an instant, I was hurled over, my stomach in knots as hot acid rose in my throat. All I'd eaten today was two slices of toast but that seemed to be enough content to vomit up onto the floor. I won't disclose what the photo depicts in this document but what I will say was that it's a situation no child of that age should ever be in. My eyes itch and then the tears begin to swell. I try to pull myself together and scoop the file back up off the desk. The man who burned here that day was a monster. But why was the folder marked and left here? Was it on purpose, did someone... Did she want it to be found?

I make my way out of the classroom just to clear my head, the trail continues with more seared footprints. Though now the flames were less controlled, swirling up the walls and across the ceiling. This very route is the last we saw from the videotape...was she holding the camera? Was she on fire? I shouldn't even be considering any of this knowing the fact I could be done for trespassing. In a blur, I charge my way through to the fire exit. It's padlocked. I turn and make it out over an empty window and across the fields behind the school property. To be honest, I don't think a single thought went through my head back then, I was on autopilot. Another feeling stops me in my tracks, fast enough to make my heart jolt.

A young voice whispers 'Did you see her? Did you see her?!'

I must've passed through a park without realising. At first, I presume they are on about me.

Another 'I told you she's real!' or maybe they are playing a game?

'She is! I just saw her! She went into the forest, the fire girl!'

I can't help myself; I retrace my steps and approach the group. What are they doing out so late?

'Where did she go?' I ask.

My voice sounded as though I was a parent going along with the make-belief. One of the little girls step back and turn away from me but in her defence, I was a stranger, a sweaty, out of breath stranger. Still, she simply points towards an opening to the forest behind the park. Walking in that direction, I follow the belief that somehow, that child's make-believe lines up with what I'm investigating. As I approach the tree line, new footprints emerge, blackened coal tracks leading between gently seared trees. The forests here always made me uneasy. As I step into the forest, the air fills with glow flies, orange hues that hang in bunches quite low to the ground. I realise once my tired eyes focus that they aren't flies at all. They're embers. Floating up from the crisp ground, following my movements deeper into the pitch-black woods. Beyond the trees, a flame dances between the shadows.

Surely, I'm dreaming again. Surely, I've inhaled some weird fumes in that school and passed out. But before I know it, there she is. A roaring fire, though the trees she stands aren't set alight. I can barely make her out from under the flames, a small girl, or what is left of her. She's scared... tired and hurt... and like a deer, in the headlights, she stares through me, and I know in my heart that if I were to step forward, she'd flee. So, I simply place her school file on the charred leaves below and take a few meters back, in each step I take back, she takes one forward.

'I'm sorry, no one found it... no one knew what he did.' I find myself talking, softly and out of my control.

'I tried to show them...but they ran away.' The sounds from her were so timid and small. She must be talking about the workers who abandoned the site.

A hand slowly traces over the folder and with a swift motion, it burns in her grasp, leaving nothing.

In a whisper 'Thank you.'

The tears that roll down her cheeks extinguish the remaining flickers of flame. Frozen and speechless, I struggle to watch as the ashy spirit blows away leaving me shrouded in the darkness once again. But just in a final

flash, a cruel aura lingers, looking for me without eyes...

then it prances into the air and out of sight. It was time to

go home.

CASE FILE NOTES:

I didn't go back to Malcolm's for a while after this, at least

he didn't mention anything. I still couldn't convince myself

that I wasn't dreaming or hallucinating from some

mysterious fumes in the school.

All I remember after this was returning home and sitting on

the porch with my dad. He asked why I was covered in soot

and dry mud, but I said I was just cleaning for Malcolm. He

didn't ask much more, he's always been quite quiet around

me, I think he's too scared to say something wrong like the

dads on TV. No questions, just a glance and a smoke.

I shouldn't be too personal here, but I want to keep a note about that night. I love my dad; he shows me the right way for all the wrong reasons. Even though he lets me get on with things without any fuss I sometimes wish that he'd give me that push. Not like mum, completely volatile. It's best with her just to keep it simple and nod my head. Since my dad has been out of work he's lost his focus. He doesn't even go out. Even though I'm out most of the time, it's noticeable. I blurted out that name, the name spooled out of me, and it was too late to go back. The cold and sad gaze painted a very clear picture; Don't say another word. You didn't need to even hear him say it. All I could come up with, are more questions and no answers. Who else knew about this fire, this girl Alicia and God knows where else this horrible story goes?!

But someone here is still hoping for their little girl to come home. A whole town hushed by a tragedy like this makes no sense. If someone was able to record the event and it ends up in cold storage without anyone from what I can tell reporting this, how and why more importantly is Malcolm sitting out on this? Out of all the junk that's been sitting here for God knows how long, we have a chance to do something important. I can tell that he doesn't see it that way, and I don't think that we'll be sorting this out tonight.

Chapter Three

ACollection of Interviews Conducted by Lindsay Baxendale.

After the chaos of my inquiry, Malcolm has decided I should step back from the archives for now and collect a series of interviews to celebrate our upcoming carnival. He mentioned that several individuals had gotten in touch about his work, claiming they could contribute to the town's history. Today, I hope to find some unique perspectives on Maere Vale.

EDITED INTERVIEW 00.00-04.12:

L: This is Lindsay Baxendale, conducting our first interview on Maere Vale's 437th year of settlement; September fifteenth. On this lovely late summer morning, we have…

C: Oh...uh, Charlie. Charlie Harrowkin.

NOTE: Charlie seems nervous...he's a tall slender lad. Perhaps he would have been more comfortable conducting this at home.

L: Hello Charlie! I believe you saw our advertisement in college and got in touch to tell us about your grandfather? Is that correct?

Inaudible

C: Contacted him about a year ago now...thought he was just ignorin' me. I- I'm glad you turned up though... I do think this is important to his research. You see, I was goin' through my grandma's stuff – me Mam told me to, you see - I found this old photo album.

My Mum was born when my grandma was only seventeen, out of wedlock 'n' all that so she was kept a secret, raised as her little sister. <Coughing> Anyway, yeah, I was goin' through the pictures, didn't know what I was lookin' for but me Mam told me something big before she passed away, was around a year an' a half ago now. -

NOTE: He can't seem to stay still, it does seem like whatever he's found has him on constant edge. The ruffling in the leather couch is somewhat distracting.

L: Oh, I'm sorry to hear that... What did she tell you?

C: Yeah thanks, wasn't much we could do to stop it, like...but yeah. I'll tell you that after.

Inaudible

C: Well, you see, I was lookin' through these photos 'n' noticed somethin', around the time my grandma turned eighteen. Took me a bit longer than that but you see, there's this guy in her birthday photo, an older guy. I think he must have been my great-granddads mate. Anyway, this guy just kinda keeps appearing, you know, in nearly all the photos. Not like in a 'you're friends with my Pa' kinda way either. He's just there.

NOTE: Charlie still hasn't shown me the pictures yet. He's been holding the album this whole time, bouncing it on top of his knees, his knuckles are white from gripping it so tightly.

L: Can I s-

C: It's weird, ya' know? He's just there. He's only next to her in one photo with her, at her birthday, that is. All the rest, he's just...around. But you see, what's weird. -

NOTE: Charlie leaned closer at this point like he was excited to tell me, but his eyes weren't excited, no, they were scared.

-C: He's always lookin' at her. My grandma. No matter where he is in the photo, he's lookin' right at her! Weird, yeah?

L: Are you sure? Maybe you've not had the chance to find out about their relationship.

C: No…

NOTE: Charlie's tone got very solemn with that answer.

C: He's *always* looking at her. I'll show you.

NOTE: Charlie puts the book on the coffee table, and flicks a few pages in.

C: This is her birthday. That's the guy next to her. Then that's her Pa.

L: I...I know...

<Audio cut off; recorder powering down>

NOTE: I must apologise for the missing part of the transcript. I had to cut the interview for a moment to collect myself.

Synopsis of missed audio: Upon seeing the photograph, I realised the man photographed was my grandfather who had died before I was born. I was able to only find two or three photographs to complete my family tree, I'm fairly certain my dad still has a copy of the one Charlie showed me. Charlie seemed just as shocked as I did and proceeded to flick through pages of photographs with him in, wanting to make sure I was right. Sadly, I was.

<Clicking and static, recorder powering on>

Edited Interview Two 00.04-3.12:

L: <Clears throat> Wow. So as of last year, you have lived in three different centuries? What was it like growing up before the war?

?: Thank you, my dear, I love a good cup of tea I do. You don't happen by chance to have any biscuits, I like digestives.

L: Oh, um, I think there's a chance we have some kept somewhere. I'll go and have a look.

Inaudible

?: That's fine, yes bring them here… I asked for a bloody biscuit.

Inaudible

?: Nothing dear!

L: So, Janey –

J: Janice.

L: Janice. Sorry. You've lived in Maere Vale your whole life?

J: I have.

L: And you want to tell me about the changes, how it has grown?

J: Grown? I wouldn't go that far. I'd say it's been an interesting place to stay in.

L: To stay in? It's no city, nor even a proper town but it's our home, right?

J: I guess so.

L: Do you loo-

J: Why did you come back?

L: I'm sorry?

J: You left, didn't you? Chance to make something of yourself.

L: Well, uh, yes I did. Things didn't… How d-

J: Well, you've buggered it now.

L: Right. Did you attend this year's celebrations?

J: No.

L: Guessed it.

J: Instead of being a rude little girl maybe you could think why.

L: Well… I have no idea. It's a great day out for families.

J: Wouldn't that be nice? Except, they haven't lived here long enough to know what it's like.

L: Well Jane- Janice, people all over the world want to better themselves.

J: I don't mean that! I'm talking about you know what. Oh, heavens I'm too old for all this.

L: Do you mean that feeling? Like when you have a moment to think to yourself and you feel everything is watching you, judging you.

J: And what if it was?

L: Why? Why does it feel like that?

J: Take it from me, some things are best left alone. Sleepy dogs lie and that.

L: Sleeping.

J: Yes, sleepy.

L: Sleepy...

J: Sleepy...

L: Well th-

\<Audio cut off; recorder powering down\>

Chapter Four

It's fascinating what you can find online now. I think that one day we'll all have our very own blog. I'm surprised there are so many people willing to share such intricate details like their favourite local record shop or job! I've even seen a few that share their real name. Just before I moved back to Maere Vale it had its own webpage set up. Whoever's running it has a questionable eye for what's noteworthy. Usually, when I'm having one of those long nights, I end up sitting in the hall on the family computer back on our webpage trying to sift through the cryptic set of what's been updated. On the first few occasions, I suspected that Malcolm was running the site as a way to backup and present his work, but it seems that even that wouldn't explain the endless articles that sprawl from intricate diagrams of local caves to the family fun run coming up. He's a bit out there but not that far. You never know what you'll find, and I guess that's the point. It's not exactly my way of winding down but it is sweet to see what's left of our community and what's not...

Talking about that fun run, there's an anniversary tribute to one of the previous winners stretched awkwardly down the sides of every page. I think the wacky fun run scheme of balloon lettering with an animated confetti explosion wasn't the most tasteful way to remember Thomas Litatio, but I'm guessing it was 'artistic liberty'. At the bottom of his page, a public guestbook is embedded. You would expect to find thoughtful condolences, maybe a message from his family, but nothing of the sort was left. An empty white box fills the screen, waiting for a response. I shouldn't be the first, I can't be? I refresh the page and my worries are bolstered. Five whole years and not a word. To die so young is one thing, but to be forgotten, that truly stings.

I did some digging and found he'd gone missing whilst training for that year's race and was last seen jogging down the narrow pass that borders the Cecil estate, just off the main road going out towards Union Road. I'm able to search records up using our new database to see if there's any other mention of Thomas just out of curiosity. Nope. Blank. It's a real shame that, pardon my phrase, his websites buried. Winners are known to go on and support a local club, even doing big charity events. I can even look at the back pages of the site and view revisions. Oddly, it's always stayed the same. Right from the first alert of his disappearance. Sounds to me like we're missing a few steps. Scrap that, there is something that has been scrubbed. A downloadable video titled 'TRAIN1.MPG' contains metadata that links it back to this page. Unfortunately, there's no chance of recovering it now. The digital humming flicks and spits as I run a final test that fills me with the giddiness of finding one more present under the

Christmas tree. Spat back to me is a single string, a sentence that doesn't need to be read to be understood. A link. A blog. An answer. A time capsule in the formless shape of a training diary. The webpage itself laid bare the dates, from February 11th 1996, all the way to September 18th 1998. Everything from diet plans to training routes was put on. All of it is still here, waiting. A photographer has captured Thomas on one of his fun runs, the caption reads: **'Speedy Gonzales! My NEW run route through our gorgeous grounds at Cecil manor'**. Nothing out of the ordinary. Let's see the first entry. I scroll through backwards in time. A map of Maere Vale, another victory lap around the market street, cheesy smiles with the fancy-dress runners, a poignant pose to inspire us all. In between the photographs, Thomas builds a clean picture of his commitments to local events. But judging by the dates it seems that the frequency to up his game is not enough. There's this ongoing diary series about Cecil manor...

April 9th, 1996: Dry but chilly conditions this morning, early start. Malt loaf, yoghurt, and cornflakes what a perfect start. If you're lucky you might even spot the red deer outside the Vale Park. You'll have to go a little off the beaten path but if you follow my NEW run route, you'll reach a loop around that takes you past our Cecil Manor. The grounds are only open to the public on our fun run in September so make sure you sign up today, you don't want to miss out!

June 19th, 1996: Did you see the beautiful sunrise this morning? Glorious! I have some fantastic news to share with our local fun run squad, this year we will be granted access to a brand-new route through Cecil Manor for this year's carnival run! But, and it's a big but, we won't be able to without your support. Make sure to show your interest by signing up before the end of next month, we need to show all our love and appreciation to the Cecil family for hosting such a memorable event every year! Until next time, RUN!

September 28th, 1996: W-O-W! What a day! We have been blessed to have had such a successful carnival this year. Did you get the chance to see Mrs Hancock's year five's production? This year the class recreated the much-loved story 'Digging Deep Down'. I'm sure you all remember franticly begging mum and dad to help with your gifting basket all those years ago... Well, it was a while ago for me! Ha Ha! Until next time, RUN!

December 31st, 1996: R.I.P To all those lost in the horrific tragedy at our very own Vale primary. No family should be spending their Christmas like this. In times like this, we must come together to remember what it means to be part of a community, to look out for one another. To keep in touch with a neighbour. To write a card to a friend you haven't seen in a while. To do the things you love with pride. I lost a very good friend too. How could something like this happen? Many have suffered and we must go into the new year with hope and the wishes that the coming days will be easier. The sadness may not end but the sun will rise and we will learn to live again.

March 4th, 1997: We need your help! This year we will be raising funds for the Vale justice families. As you all know, this is a cause close to my heart and I'm sure for many of you it is so too. You may also know that the council has decided that the new budget will not support reopening the school nor open further inquiries into the roots of that terrible disaster. That is why we need you to do the right thing. I'm aware we don't have many visitors to the blog, but I believe even one person can make a difference... That person could be you. Please find the time to get in touch and give what you can to support our families, our town, and our run. Thank you.

September 20th, 1997: It is with great sadness that I am announcing the cancellation of this year's fun run.

Throughout my time at Maere Vale's celebrations, I have been able to contribute my part to showcasing the real spirit of dedicated charity and the freedom running can give to each and every one of us. Young and old, fast, and slow. It is not just about training to win; it's about being part of something together. With this blog, I was hoping to find new connections with others in the community who wanted to share their love for our town and the love it gives back. Slowly that has turned out to be a fruitless effort. Perhaps it's easier if we just forget about our history. Give up on the challenges. Stop turning out, shut ourselves away. No one watching, no one will remember.

September 18th, 1998: Through the trees, you will see. A home calling for you and me. Don't ignore it, shall not stand it. Breakaway from the buzz and the speed, a place you know, does it mean much to me? Further, I go. A new beginning, no more lingering. Do you hear it? Ignore it? Challenge it? Life will throw those questions and you shall make a choice. A world ever-growing, that no one will reach for. Not for me. Into the garden, the green and the glow. Anywhere but here, inside they'll be no fear, we will have comfort in the chaos. Somewhere warm and away, far, far away.

Note: I think that's everything I can salvage. Now that we have a permanent record there's a possibility that we'll eventually shed some light on what happened to Thomas Litatio. One thing is for sure, the next step is Cecil Manor.

Needing answers, I make my way to Cecil Manor itself. Long before Thomas' disappearance, the Manor had been closed to the public, after a dispute in inheritance ownership from demands all over the world. The first inheritors had moved from an unspecified location in Europe during the 1850s. Secluded; the family had kept to themselves for generations. Despite the image, we see today the town shunned them. To improve relations the family would host an annual ball during the autumn period, inviting their home to the community. Over the years, more would turn up and spend their time making snide comments, even though the parties were more lavish than anyone else could offer. Tales of desperate attempts to seem unpleased and avoid the hosts till existing to this day although conflicting accounts said the hosts were never actually present. I have brought the available archived letters and newspapers to compare the only descriptions of the original owners of Cecil Manor and its grounds. Letters would triumph over the townspeople's opinions on the newcomers, how they looked so different with their jet-black hair, sharp features, and eyes so dark they appeared to have no reflection. Even the papers would note how strange this family was. Looking further into the newspapers, I've noticed that at least once a year, around the same time as the annual ball, a person would be reported missing. It's possible that the day Thomas went missing matches the same day as the annual ball hosted by the original owners. Not only that but I also think Malcolm

mentioned we no longer celebrate at the Cecil Manor

during the autumn festival. The final bit of information I

was able to find was from the Modern Domesday record for

the house. A mother, father and son are born the year after

the first party. No other record corroborates this

information and considering the missing cases we have a

serious matter on our hands. I don't think this is a matter

for Malcolm anymore...

I still can't believe that he's shying away from all of this. I

feel like this is my last shot at trying to get answers. I've

run our resources dry and to be honest breaking and

entering isn't my thing!

Thomas' route takes me up to the Eastward side of the

manor. It's hard to believe that tucked away along a lonely,

unmarked path a baroque house awaits me. The vantage

point from an eroding mossy wall is going to require me to

do a bit of climbing. Wasn't quite what I had in mind a

runner would be doing each morning, so I hope this is worth it. I holster my bag onto the top of the wall, misjudging it I hear it tumble down the other side, leaving me with no choice. I clutch onto the highest possible jittered piece of rock, just a few inches from the top. Every few seconds pausing to let out another yawn louder than the last. With one last yank, I roll onto the top. This... I see it now. In full view, a sleepy grand house. Perhaps deep in there are my answers. The final place is described by Thomas, an alluring mystical place. Were we told as kids about this house? Such history that it must tell! The first signs of a creeping sun from the opposite side spotlight the trimmed snaking garden and its cobbled drive. There aren't any cars and from here it looks like all the curtains are drawn. An intense need to run away begins to bubble. I swallow it down and make my way through the garden and along the outside of the manor until I can get a better look at one of the high windows… left open. The sturdy rose lattice should do the trick.

Oh wow. My first impression is that this is being kept in its original state aside from a few glass cabinets with what I think are bottles of wine and the low chandeliers using lightbulbs. For the record, there are two rooms immediately to my right and one to the left. You can easily imagine you are living here in town some hundred and fifty years ago and you're invited to a place like this. Somewhere you wouldn't even be able to dream of. Who would not be jealous? The bright and broad lavish house is all for three people, not a hint of any problems and you are there to believe that all this land is needed whilst your struggles grow with every passing winter. Fewer crops, less trade. Yes, that's right, this is simply an unofficial tour guide. If you saw this room you would know it is exactly like what I'd read. I can confirm that there is a bedroom for the son mentioned. The papers state that over the years the family became even more secluded, sending their 'unfortunate' house servants to do their shopping from the closest town.

This next door could lead to the master bedroom on the left side of the corridor. This room has a sort of misery about it, a sense of being more abandoned than the other rooms. I pace around the room, going over to the untouched bed that smells like dust, the sheets have faded, and the wallpaper is losing its pattern. Then over to a vanity, the makeup upon it is still intact and the perfume bottle still has liquid in it. In the drawer, a small diary with a key tied to the fabric bookmark. I slip it into my jacket without hesitation. Such a strange bottle of perfume, I idly fumble with it as I walk around the rest of the room. Then comes the wardrobe, which is built into the wall, upon opening it, a variety of hand-tailored garments spool out. I accidentally spray the perfume and as the liquid sprays towards the inside of the wardrobe, a breeze pushes the plume back towards me.

'A breeze?'

Putting the bottle aside, I part the heavy clothing to inspect the wall behind it. With my torch in my mouth, I'm able to run my hands over the wall until I feel that there is a hollow section beneath the wallpaper. I push against the bottom until the top board is forced forwards, splitting the paper slightly. I rip away the paper and break off the plank of wood and see that there is a hallway. After breaking away enough wood, I venture down the passage until I come to a door. A locked door. A rather small keyhole for a door. Would you believe me if I told you that the diary key fits? Inside, there's another bedroom. Even more so, this room is sorrowful. I scan the room and notice a door to the right which is confusing as there was only one door on this side of the corridor. But this door is sealed shut. Before exploring any further, I rest on a chair by the door and pull out the diary. What a find! Simply signed, 'the lady of the house'.

Note: The diary was found in a poor condition, and I disclose that its full details cannot be recorded.

January 2nd, 1855

We are settled. An unwelcome beginning for certain, yet our peace shall be made not found. Now, I can picture a day when our Stefan will hold my hand and describe to me the beautiful flowers that I have tended for him. He shall sit at the table and celebrate our endurance to finding a world for us, built by us. A fresh beginning, for a family that deserves more. My mother would scold me for the mere suggestion, but I concur that despite the disorder of our old life we must strive for a better day. We will teach the people to embrace us, to understand us. We are human too.

Note: Most of the diary is inventory and upkeep entries for goods and pay to the servants of the house. Crucially, we have a suggestion that there were witnesses to what happened here...

- Excerpt from an Unknown Take 00.00:00.56 –

I hate him. I fucking hate him. It's not some 'little
adventure'. He actually hit me. Something is very wrong.
I'm not even safe back here, I'm supposed to be home. And
now I stand up for myself, I see through the lies. I don't
have anyone. Maybe.

I come across some scrawled, more distressed handwriting,
a lot of it is blurred by blots of water damage. This entry is
just questions, despair, and rage. They'd snatched her boy;
they'd hurt him and taken them away from her. She'd lost
her son to the cruelty of the townspeople after they'd
attacked him. How can such a thing happen? He'd snuck
out as he disagreed with how his parents thought they
should just keep to themselves and never return. Unable to
read any more, for now, I slam the book shut and finish the
search. After a short while, I learn this is the son's room

and the parents must have sealed it off after he died, it looks more like a hospital ward. The four-poster bed is mangled with layers of sheets and dried up towels. Bowls underneath the bed have formed a hazy ooze on top. Letter sheets sprawl on the bedside desk. From a woman, a farmer's daughter in fact. Love. I shall only disclose that this loping was perhaps the trigger to the folks' rage.

Leaving the room and continuing to read the diary in small sections, I end up at the final entry. The mother's grief has changed. She begins to talk about the possibility of saving her son and bringing him back to her. She had only one friend in this town: her head maid. Her maid spoke of how the town had a vein of magic running through it, how her grandmother would tell her stories of a spell that could bring you what you desired. A plan is made to make a sacrifice to bring her son back. An all too familiar date is mentioned, September 14th. Just as I work this out, singing comes from behind a large door at the end of the corridor.

That must be the ballroom. As I approach the ballroom, the music grows louder, and the sound of chatter and footsteps can be heard. I slowly ease the door open to find a blank room. In the final pages, the mother declares that the summoning magic had worked, that this dark spirit arose and swam into her heart. It was the soul of her son. Or at least she said it was.

It demanded her to acquire a vessel for him to possess, his corpse was... useless. It is at this point that the yearly ball began. First, the family who killed her son had plenty of their own to spare. The least they could do is replace her son. Though after the first boy was collected, the mother spun into a rage that resulted in his death too. A rage she couldn't control, whatever had possessed her did this. He deserved a better body; didn't she want her son to be happy? To have the perfect body. After this, the rage being taken out on her wore her down, she became weaker. As the years passed, the same was repeated until the mother was crippled and worn down to her bone. The father had left, unable to bear with how his wife was behaving. Every year, a ball was hosted, and a body was taken just for it to fail. They eventually were renamed the Litatio family, meaning prey, a favourable sacrifice.

As I read these final words, I end up making my way down into a basement beneath the ballroom. Until I pick up on an odd creaking beneath my feet. I brush away the rubble and dust and discover a trap door.

Down here I fear for the worst. There are two creatures...one a blurred reflection of the mother, the other...indescribable, ominous, and hungry...I cannot understand what they are trying to say, the mother weeping like a banshee, the other... Whatever had possessed her those centuries ago still consumes what has left; this grief-stricken spirit who'd been alluring men to this property in some desperate way to bring her son back, even long after her death. This creature had sucked the life out of her and here it was to finish the job. It must be hungry to return to such old prey. As they wailed at one another, I only now see the floor piled in bone. The evil lets out a final wail and destroys what was left of the mother.

Then it turned its attention to me, frozen. Still, it is hungry. It shall consume like it has to countless beings and uses her to do unspeakable things to quench its thirst.

… I don't remember what happened next, as I came around after passing out on the floor, I heard Malcolm's voice.

'Run! Run! Get out of here, now!'

Clawing its way through the clothes the creature screams. Malcolm's veins swell and his skin turns grey as it binds itself to him. Malcolm, with pain in his eyes, screams for me to run. But I can't. I know what to do now.

'Why would you come here? Lindsay, you can't tell anyone about this.' Malcolm struggles to push out each word.

'Malcolm! You- you wanted me to do this. We could have done this together!'

'What? And end up here? What good can that do? Go, now. Please.'

'Please Malcolm, I'll help you.'

His body was now immeasurably heavy. The fat sacks pull him to the floor. With my strength, I manage to drag him to the top of the basement stairs. But it is too late. He is weary and weak.

'Malcolm. Malcolm. Get on the bed, Malcolm.'

'Lock the door, Lindsay.'

'But.'

'You have to.'

'I'm sorry Malcolm.'

Final Note

- Excerpt from Take One 24.16:26.31 -

And so here we are today. I have packed up Malcolm's shed. Most of his things will be destroyed but I hope that this record stands that one day you will finish the job. It's up to you now. The truth is out there. This chaotic justice is a powerful thing. It can manifest our anger, our bitterness and our love. In that vulnerable state, the elements can react. Never forget what happened at Maere Vale. Perhaps with a little digging, you'll find your own adventure.

Moving Bodies

For the dancers, their clocks.

For our time shall now stop.

To the kiss, till it hangs and for more the same.

You watch the bloom, its blood, its songbird that still calls.

For now, the visions are recalled and the visions evermore.

Printed in Great Britain
by Amazon

82181748R00130